After Yoga

Intenseros Press

After Yoga

A Young Woman's Reluctant Journey Of Sensual Discovery

E. J. Carlucci

For information, contact Intenseros Press at:

media@intenseros.com

Book Design, Editing, and Cover Design by E. J. Carlucci

Typeface for main text is Bitstream Charter

ISBN 978-0-9891355-4-2

Contents

1

=====

THE INTRODUCTION

Everything was fuzzy when I first came to.

I was lying on my back on a padded surface, facing upward. I tried to clear the blurriness from my eyes, but quickly realized that I had no physical access to my eyes to even rub them, because my wrists seemed to be restrained. And not just restrained, but held down with my arms crossing my back-swept upper thighs where they met my buttocks.

I tested the wrist restraints, and realized that while they weren't tight, neither were they releasable; I couldn't raise them much or prevent my arms from holding back my upper legs.

And in that moment, I realized that it was not only my wrists that were restrained. The discomfort of my position created an awareness that my thighs were not just held down by my arms, but that they were even more restricted, by my lower legs; my ankles seemed to be stuck together behind my head.

This wasn't a novel posture for me; I had often practiced it as part of my private yoga routine to flex and stretch, and occasionally I'd done it during sex to please a guy. But I'd never before had my feet behind my head without being able to release myself from that position.

I had often been complimented on the proportions of my body, but I'd always wished that my legs were longer, and I'd never wished it so much as I did now – my torso spreading and bending my knees, they didn't allow me to get my feet back over my head, as long as they were connected, regardless of how much I stretched and strained to do so.

The fear at my circumstances started to bubble up within me, but I tried not to panic, and instead continued to assess my situation, wondering just what I'd gotten myself into.

I had of course assumed from the beginning that it would involve some sort of sexual activity, but the contract hadn't been very specific about exactly what was to happen to me, or when or how, other than that I wouldn't be physically injured, and that I'd have a safe phrase, with the proviso that the use of it would void the agreement. But I had filled out a questionnaire about what I was willing and unwilling to do. So it seemed interesting.

I hadn't been sure whether I could trust them to pay, but I'd been referred by a girlfriend who'd refused to give me any details, saying only that I'd find it unforgettable, and that any foreknowledge on my part would spoil the experience for everyone. So since I generally liked sex as long as it wasn't too kinky, I'd signed it anyway; five thousand dollars was a lot of money for a barista with student loans.

As I lay there, restrained and still a little woozy, I cast my mind back to the events that had resulted in this predicament, just a few hours ago. Or more, or less; it was hard to know, as I didn't know what time or even day it now was, because I had no idea how long I'd been out from the drugs.

I had just left my normal yoga workout, in my normal post-workout clothes – yoga pants, sweatshirt, and sandals – when I heard a voice behind me.

"Ms. Katsaros."

The tone and inflection indicated that it wasn't a question; it was more of a command.

I turned around and saw a tall blonde woman, her apparently abundant hair put up in a large chignon. She would have looked somewhat like Elsa from *Frozen* if, instead of resplendent in a regal-blue dress, the Disney princess had been immaculately attired in a well-tailored charcoal-gray conservative business suit, with knee-length skirt revealing well-formed calves leading down to black three-inch heels.

As I was taking in her appearance, she in turn looked me slowly up and down, seemingly disapprovingly, for a few seconds, and then announced, in a crisp, upper-class English accent, "We have examined your application for our lucrative temporary position, and would like to provisionally offer it to you. However, before consummating the contract, we require a final personal interview."

In my current financial straits, this seemed like good news.

"When would the interview be scheduled?"

"Immediately.

"You will come with me now."

The tone of her response would clearly brook no disagreement.

"I was supposed to meet a friend for coffee after yoga."

"Text him or her, and tell them that something has come up.

"In fact, you will set up an auto-reply for incoming texts that you will be out of cell range for the next day or two, so no one will worry about you if you miss any messages."

I frowned, but then pulled my phone out of my purse and texted Sara that an emergency had come up, and that I'd explain later, and I texted my boss at the coffee shop that I might not be there in the morning. Then I set up the autoreply as she had demanded; I didn't want to lose this opportunity.

"All right, let's go."

She had turned around with the words, and was walking quickly down the street. I ran to catch up with her.

"Where are we going?"

"Not far."

"Will it take long?"

"No, but believe me, it will be thorough."

She spoke no further, though she tapped at her phone, as we continued to rapidly move along. After a minute or so, we turned into a parking lot a half block away, and approached a black limousine. The right rear door was open. An exotically beautiful Asian-looking woman of medium height, in a chauffeurs' uniform, including black hair bundled under the cap, was standing by it.

"Get in, and sit in the rear seat, across from her," she briskly commanded.

I looked inside, and hesitated as I saw a woman in a white nurse's uniform sitting in the rear-facing seat at the other side of the car, with a doctor's satchel beside her.

Then I slowly climbed in, set my purse on the floor, and sat down as ordered, facing her.

I could see the word "NORA" on the uniform badge. She had pretty features, with shoulder-length auburn hair.

The blonde woman followed me in, and sat on the rear-facing seat along with the nurse, if she indeed was one, and the door was closed behind her. A few seconds later I heard a clunk as the doors locked. I reached over to test one, and realized that it was locked from the inside as well, with no release button.

"We don't want to be disturbed," she explained, seeing the concerned expression on my face but continuing to be expressionless herself. "We also don't want you to leave prematurely, before we have finished the procedure."

"I used the word 'interview,' but in a sense, the application and preference form was the interview. Really, this is more of a physical examination to determine your fitness for whatever exertions we will demand of you. This woman is a registered nurse, who will perform the exam."

"It doesn't seem like a typical medical clinic," I remarked.

"It will serve." The nurse's voice had a husky, sexy tone.

"And is it standard practice for you to have a non-medical professional participate?"

The blonde woman spoke up.

"Ms. Katsaros, there are many young women eager for the opportunity to do what we have chosen you to do, some perhaps who would do it for even less money. They are available to us even today. One more impertinent and disrespectful comment like that and we will unlock the door, release you, and give your lucrative opportunity to one of them, whom I am sure would greatly appreciate it. Am I clear?"

Chastened, and fearing losing the gig, I nodded.

"I am on the verge of making a significant business investment in what I hope will be a valuable commodity. It would be fiduciarily irresponsible to my business to do so without personally inspecting the merchandise."

I internally bristled at being callously characterized as "merchandise" but, given the amount of money, I could see her point.

"All right," the nurse announced. "We will start with your blood pressure and pulse. Roll up your left sleeve."

As I rolled up the sleeve on my sweatshirt, she got out a wrist-cuff monitor and velcroed it on me, then pushed the button. The pump started and I felt the pressure on my wrist, and then a slight pain in my arm as the circulation was momentarily cut off. It counted down to the result, and then I heard and felt the pressure released.

"130/90, and pulse of 88. A little high for someone of her age and build, but not necessarily an issue; probably a result of nervousness at the circumstances."

The blonde woman nodded in apparent understanding.

The nurse put away the device, then moved her face very close into mine, staring silently and deeply into my widened brown eyes with her own hazel ones for a few seconds longer than seemed comfortable. She finally spoke, slowly.

"The physical exam itself will start at the top..." she paused, and then opened her mouth and gently licked my closed lips a few times, "...and work our way down to...the bottom." She backed off.

"Now open your mouth, and let's see your tongue."

I blinked a couple times, and shook off the seeming spell, then slowly obeyed her as she came at me with a tongue depressor and bright light. She pressed the depressor down. "Say 'ah.'"

As I vibrated my vocal chords, she looked down my throat with the light.

"Throat and uvula seem pink and healthy. Keep the tongue stuck out as far as you can."

Setting down the instruments, her face once again approached my own with the tongue still extended from my mouth, and her eyes stared deeply again into mine for a few seconds. Then, closing them as if to concentrate, she slowly stuck her own tongue out and, to my shock, gently licked the end of mine with it, slowly rotating around it, almost in a minuet, then stroking back and forth on the top and bottom, for almost ten seconds. Strangely, though I had never done anything sexual with a woman, I found it arousing, albeit bizarre.

Opening her eyes and withdrawing her tongue to speak, she explained, "How a tongue tastes has a surprising amount of clues to physical health. Based on my experience, I detected nothing out of the ordinary, other than garlic and onions."

"Panera for lunch."

"All right, time to check out your heart. Off with the sweatshirt."

I hesitated, then seeing the look in the eyes of the blonde woman on whose good graces I currently depended, slowly reached down, pulled the bottom up, and over my head. I pulled first one arm, then the other through and set the shirt down on the seat beside me.

"Bra, too."

I slowly reached up and unclipped the front, separated the cups, then pulled my arms through and removed it, setting it on top of the sweatshirt. My large bare breasts were now on full display to the two women.

She raised the ear pieces of a stethoscope that had been resting on her shoulders, and put them into her ears. "I hate cold stethoscopes. I have a theory that the shock of the chill on the chest or the breast affects the heart rate. So I've been keeping this one body temperature for you."

She reached into the uniform and removed the chest piece that had apparently been resting against her own bare bosom under the blouse. She then reached forward, cupped and lifted my left breast in her left hand, and pressed the chest piece against the upper part of it. It was pleasantly warm as she had said, and I tried to breathe calmly as she listened for several seconds.

"Now close your mouth, breathe very deeply a few times, then cough." She continued to listen as I obeyed.

Finally, she pulled it away. "The heart rate continues to be somewhat elevated, but again, that's not unexpected under the circumstances. I hear no arrhythmia or abnormality. Her cardiac function seems normal, and her heart strong. No obvious lung issues either."

Though she then took off the stethoscope and set it aside, she continued to weigh my breast in her hand.

"Yes, 36D if it's an ounce. No need to measure; she seems to have been honest on her application."

"Yes," the blonde woman replied. "Despite her hideous attire, I was admiring her curves and body proportions on the sidewalk. Her self reports do seem accurate."

Continuing to hold my breast, with her other hand, she gently brushed the backs of her fingertips around my nipple. "She has nice large aureoles. I think the patrons will find that quite aesthetically pleasing."

I didn't speak, but the sensation of her fingers on my sensitive breast end felt very good. But what happened next was both more pleasurable, and disturbing. She gently grasped the nub with her fingers, and started to squeeze it and brush it directly. As she did so, I could feel it start to swell and harden in them, sending a little sparkle up my spine. She could feel the hardening as well.

"Observe how responsive the nipple is to manipulation. The blood flows readily to it, and I suspect that's not the only place the blood is flowing to. Let's see if she's symmetrical."

She released the left breast, letting it drop, and picked up and squeezed the other one, whereupon she started similar ministrations of its own nipple, which responded in a similar manner. Despite my fear, and previous belief that I was totally straight, I was starting to get sexually excited by what this woman was doing to me and, as she had implied, the blood was flowing to engorge the sexual organs between my clothed legs as well. After a minute or so, as it continued to swell, she released it, too.

"All right, put the bra and shirt back on," I heard, to my relief; I wasn't to be stripped completely naked in front of these strange women. I put on the bra, and then pulled the sweatshirt back over my head. But the feeling was short lived.

"We'll keep working our way downward, to check out the health and appearance of the money makers. Time to peel off those tight pants."

2

THE SEDUCTION AND ABDUCTION

Momentarily frozen in fear and embarrassment at the nurse's command to remove my pants, but seeing again the blonde woman's steely gaze, I finally pulled off my sandals, then reluctantly leaned forward, lifted my behind from the seat, and started to slowly stretch and pull the waist seam past my hips, and down to the floor of the car. I lifted first one leg, then the other out of them, and put them on the seat next to me as I had previously with the sweatshirt and bra. I was now sitting on the limousine seat wearing a sweatshirt, but nothing below my waist except my underwear.

"You know what to do next."

I sighed, then raised myself again, and rolled the panties down to my ankles, stepping out of them.

"All right, for your examination, you are going to put the pants on the floor, and lie on your stomach on the seat, face sideways toward the front of the vehicle. You will bend your left knee and rest the lower leg against the door. Your right leg will go down to the floor over the edge of the seat, bent at the hip."

With the commands, which were clearly not requests, she laid a towel on the seat where she apparently wanted my hips to go.

I slowly obeyed, wondering if the money was really going to be worth this. I knew that in that sexy, almost seductive position, everything between my now-naked legs would be completely exposed to the women, and particularly the blonde woman who was sitting right there. But part of me, still aroused from the previous breast massage, was now also perversely excited about it.

As I lay there, the upper part of my slightly swollen bare clitoris now pressing against the towel, fearing what would come next, the nurse moved over and gently grabbed the cheeks of my buttocks and spread them apart.

She silently held me wide with her hands for several seconds, and then finally observed, "The hair appears to be roughly the same dark brunette color at both ends of her body. She doesn't seem to dye it – it is probably the natural color. The vulva appears to be pink and healthy.

"Beyond that, it is quite lovely in form. The outer vaginal lips are plump, and slightly swollen from my breast massages and the general psychological tension of the situation, but not so much so as to hide the symmetrical inner lips, which are slightly glistening from her arousal as I spread them apart and the vagina starts to secrete. The clitoris is usefully prominent and itself somewhat engorged from nipple squeezing, though I suspect it can get larger.

"The anus also appears healthy, and clean. It too is attractively symmetrical and round, quite likely to arouse most men who view it. The perineum is of a nice width, making for a good separation between the orifices."

I watched as the blonde woman nodded in approval to the clinical description, though there was no other sign of pleasure. Even more perversely, the words aroused me ever further.

She temporarily released the buttocks, but then I could feel her take one hand and re-spread me with thumb and fingers. Then I felt her start to gently caress the soft tender skin just outside my outer vaginal lips with the backs of the clipped fingertips of her free hand, as she had earlier with my aureoles. The tingling between my legs, now sparkling all the way up my spine, was exquisite, but I tried to remain calm, and not reveal any emotion.

She continued to softly stroke me. "Does this feel good?"

"It's OK," I lied, continuing to look with a frown toward the front of the vehicle with my head on the seat, my arms on the seat and the floor. She smiled as she continued to observe the further swelling and seeping of my increasingly aroused genitals. It was becoming more and more difficult to hold in a moan of pleasure.

She stopped momentarily, and once again grabbed and spread me wide from both sides with both hands. She put her face down deep in the cleft between the cheeks, took a deep inhalation, and then I felt her gently run her tongue up and down a few times along the middle of the moist inner lips. This time I couldn't hold back a closed-mouth "mmmmmmmmmmmm" of passion.

"She seemed to enjoy that, perhaps more than she lets on, but the primary purpose was for me to smell and taste her, to detect any genital health issues. She seems to have showered recently, but despite that, I would have noticed something if there was a problem."

"I always do right after yoga, in this case less than an hour ago." I continued to lie there, still frowning toward the front of the car, increasingly annoyed at repeatedly being referred to in the third person, as though I wasn't right there.

As she again held me spread with a single hand, I felt her take a couple fingers of the other, and insert them deep into my exposed vagina. "She is quite wet now, but I think we can get more out of her."

With the words, she withdrew the fingers, and then started to use the lubricated digits to finally directly massage my swollen clitoris below it, which quickly grew larger and harder. My eyes closed now, I softly sighed.

"Oh, fuck."

"Does that feel nice?"

"You fucking well know it does," I moaned.

As she continued to pleasure me, I got past the delicious sensations momentarily to ask, "Is this standard practice in an exam? All of my previous ones have been all business."

"In nursing school, I learned to combine business with pleasure. Not from the professors, but from my fellow students, both male and female.

"Can you give me a hand here? Or, rather, two? I need someone to spread her for me, because for the next step, I need both my own hands." The last was obviously to the blonde woman, who had been looking on with a combined expression of clinical study and fascination.

I was surprised at the incongruity of this conservatively dressed woman, without hesitation, quickly getting on her knees and taking my buttocks in her own hands, as the nurse stood back for a moment. Silent, she started to gently knead them, giving me a new sensation. She gradually started to pull them apart and then relax them, rhythmically spreading and narrowing both my outer and inner genital lips, and opening and closing my vagina. It made little clicking sounds as the now-wet seal of the entrance itself was repeatedly closed and reopened. I was starting to moan seriously now. The thumbs then moved lower, down to the clefts where my buttocks met my upper legs, and the fingers higher, adjacent to my perineum and anus, and now each forced separation spread all, widely.

"OK, now hold her open and spread for me."

As I could feel the blonde woman respond to her request, the nurse moved in and reinitiated her massage of my most sensitive sexual organ. As she did so, she dipped the fingers of her other hand into my spread-open vagina for more lubrication, and started to gently stroke the perineum above it. The dual sensation was heavenly, and I had reached a point at which I was willing to let either of them do almost anything they wanted. It continued for a deliriously delicious couple of minutes, but then the finger massaging the region between my anus and vagina slowly drifted up and gently circled the sphincter of my anus itself. Despite the almost unbearably intense pleasure, it was starting to become alloyed with fear. When the juice-slickened finger spiraled in and started to gently massage the tender skin outside the muscular orifice, my entire body stiffened. I think they could sense that they perhaps had found something they couldn't do with me.

While my last name was Katsaros, I had never really felt of Greek descent. My mother was of Spanish descent, my father's father had married someone whose parents were from Lebanon, and my paternal great-grandfather had married a woman he'd met in Little Italy. Many who knew my heritage and complimented me on my beauty had told me that it was because of this amalgam of Mediterranean pulchritude and, ignoring the unknowns of my matrilineal ancestry, I was no more than one eighth Greek.

But despite that, my last name nonetheless resulted in a lot of crude jokes growing up and, worse, as I got older, pressure from guys who insisted that because of my ancestry, however trace, I was somehow genetically predisposed, even compelled, to respond to stereotype and love to take it in the ass. This experience had determined me to start a lifelong crusade against that idiotic stereotype, particularly after one guy, whom I had stupidly cared about and tried a lot harder to keep than I should have, hurt the hell out of me trying to do it.

The survey I had filled out as part of the application was basically a list of sexual activities, with boxes for "Yes," "Meh," and "No way." I'd gone down the list, and elaborated on the simple check boxes:

Cunnilingus: Hell yes!

Vaginal Intercourse: Yay!

Lesbian: Never tried it, but YOLO.

Bondage: Sounds like it could be fun.

Breast Sucking: Bring it on!

Golden Showers: Weird, but at least let me have a non-golden one afterward.

Anal: Not only no, but HELL NO.

Enemas: See Anal.

Despite my obvious fear, she continued to massage me there. After a while, and when nothing else happened, I gradually got used to it, and even started to relax and enjoy it a little, as my clitoris continued to get harder and more sensitive with the massage, and distracting me from it. I could sense a climax coming on, and she seemed to be able to tell, as she started to speed up the motions.

I was starting to moan even louder now, leveraging my right leg on the floor to move my hips up and down and lift my groin off the towel, to allow her better access to my clitoris to increase the stimulation.

Suddenly, she took the fingers of the hand of the same thumb that had been rubbing it, and inserted them into my vagina, spreading it with them and stroking in and out. It put me over the edge, and I grunted out the sudden orgasm, uncontrollably bucking against the hands of the women behind me, then groaned as another one erupted.

The orgasms seemed to be almost non-stop, but they reached a crescendo when I felt an object suddenly slightly stretch my lubricated sphincter, and a finger thrust deep into my rectum. I screamed at the sudden shock and sur-prising ecstasy of the intrusion in my forbidden orifice, try-ing to push all of the fingers out of both of my holes with my internal muscles, almost involuntarily in my helpless passion, but now the women, who were surprisingly strong, held me down and forced me to continue to come.

After another minute or so, the stimulation ended, but the blonde woman continued to hold my hips down to the seat, cheeks still spread, and the nurse kept her finger buried deep in my ass, though she had withdrawn them from the orifice below it. As I started to recover from the spasms of pleasure, I realized that in fact it hadn't and didn't hurt, so I stopped squeezing so hard and trying to eject it, and just started to relax in that position. Then, after a while, as my sense of relaxation continued to grow, she slowly and pleasurably slid the finger out of my tightly stretched anus, to my relief.

I continued to lie there as my breaths grew less frequent, then I heard the English-accented words.

"All right, I think you've passed the physical. Dora, I believe we have a keeper." I heard the engine start, and felt the car start to move. The instant response implied that the young Asian-looking woman driver (apparently whom she had addressed) had been listening to the whole thing, which I found a little embarrassing.

"You may put your pants back on now." The words were apparently this time to me.

I continued to lie there, with a sense of post-orgasmic languor, idly wondering if I was now officially a lesbian, or at least bi. But then I realized that they'd been pleasuring me, not I them. I'd done nothing physical to them, or been attracted to them *per se*, and as far as I knew, they hadn't climaxed themselves, though I suspected they'd gotten a little excited. So I guessed that I was still heterosexual.

I slowly sat up, feeling slightly dizzy, no doubt from the exertions. I pulled on my panties, then lifted one leg to put the pants on with no problem, but the second one seemed heavier, and I was starting to feel tired. But I struggled and finally got them back on. Now sitting up, I remarked to the blonde woman, "The finger in my ass was a surprise, but it was narrow, so it didn't hurt. But I'm still glad that anal isn't included in my contract."

"Don't be ridiculous," she replied. "You signed a contract, and filled out a survey. Neither have anything to do with the other. In fact, you were chosen because you were the only applicant we've ever had who expressed interest in everything *except* anal. This information will entertainingly inform the coming performance."

Though I was increasingly relaxed, and getting sleepy, the words came as a shock. As the implications sunk in, I declared quietly, and now drowsily, "I want out."

"Under the terms of the contract, you may of course use your safe phrase at any time to end the engagement, at the cost of your compensation. And of course, the sooner you do this the better, to better cut your losses. But right now would be a little too soon. If we were to release you now, you wouldn't make it half a dozen steps before collapsing on the pavement, and perhaps injuring yourself, not to mention creating an awkward and unseemly situation for all concerned. Under the terms of our agreement, that would not be permissible.

"You see, you probably think that your relaxation and sleepiness are the result of your great orgasms, but in fact they are the result of what happened *during* the orgasms. You didn't notice at the time in your passion as you were mindlessly groaning and thrusting your lovely arse and swollen throbbing quim back against our hands, but at *that* point, as you seemed to be so exceptionally sexually responsive and good at coming, in addition to your other attractions, I'd decided to give you the job.

"I nodded to Nora and, as she had been increasingly lubricating your sphincter with your flowing and dripping cunt juices, she easily slipped the large tranquilizer capsule into your bum as you continued to come hard and were involuntarily straining and stretching its tight hole open for her. She then followed it in with her finger, to plunge it deeply into you and keep you from shooting it back out of your arse hole in your uncontrolled excitement.

"As I firmly held your bum down and kept you spread, and she continued to seal your tightly squeezing young hole with her finger for a while, first as you continued to helplessly buck, and then after you had finished coming, she had sealed your immediate fate as well.

"She had felt the passionate heat of your bowels melting and liquefying the capsule, relentlessly and inevitably releasing the powerful drugs into your intestinal lining.

"I can safely tell you this now because there is absolutely nothing at all that you can any longer do about it. You are now effectively totally under our physical control. As we speak, the drugs are coursing through your bloodstream, and the effects will become greater and greater over time until they later wear off, and quite quickly now. In fact, you already appear to be unable to any longer sit up."

With her crude description of what they had just done to me, shocking coming from the mouth of someone who had initially seemed so prim and proper, how I had been feeling suddenly made sense; I could almost sense the drugs being pumped by my heart from deep in my bowels directly into my brain. And she was right; I could no longer keep my eyes open and was starting to slump in the car seat, and almost didn't care any more. Strengthless, I felt the nurse take my upper body, and gently lay me down on it, while the blonde woman lifted my now-leaden legs and put them on the other end of the seat.

As I continued to helplessly drift off, I heard her finish, "We are going to open up new sexual horizons for you, and you will be well paid. But right now, you are going to take a little nap for us, to allow us to prepare you and what we've now seen lies between your lovely thighs for your upcoming lucrative performance. When you next awaken, it will be show time."

Other than a few immediate bumps and turns along the road, her final words were the last thing I had remembered when I had awoken.

3

=====

THE INDUCTION

Back in the frightening present, strapped down to a padded surface on my back with my feet cuffed behind my head, I wasn't sure what was about to happen to me, but if I was to believe her last words to me before I had lost consciousness, it was "show time," or about to be, whatever that meant. I continued to try to avoid panic, and to calmly assess my situation. I blinked several times to try to clear my eyes. I raised my head, and looked first at myself, and then my surroundings.

My long dark-brown hair, that I had put up in a bun before yoga and had remained up in the limousine through my "medical exam" and orgasms, was now down and splayed behind me and at my sides. I seemed to be almost totally unclothed, except for a sheer bikini top, and tight panties that I could feel on my hips and between my legs. I also felt a little strange, unfamiliar sensation from them down there, but couldn't quite put my finger on what it was, particularly since my restrained wrists literally prevented me from touching myself there with my fingers. But I could look down beyond my barely covered breasts, beyond my abdomen, to see them, the only barrier between my most private bodily parts and the open air: white and also very sheer.

And this was the most frightening thing; neither of the garments were mine.

The implications of that fact gave me a sinking feeling in the pit of my stomach; I had already been completely naked while unconscious, and I had no idea in the presence of whom, or what he or she or they had already done to me beyond removing and changing my clothing and restraining me, though I was pretty sure that the women who had abducted me had been involved.

Beyond my own body, I could see what appeared to be a small theater, with two or three dozen stadium seats, empty, in a room elaborately decorated in various shades of red and pink. On the wall above the seats were two large video monitors.

To my shock, I saw that they were both currently displaying me from above, lying on a padded red platform, wearing nothing except the tight underwear and sheer bikini top, my feet behind my head and my arms strapped down beside my lower legs with wrist restraints, with my ass hanging slightly over the edge of it. One of them was displaying a high-resolution close up of my currently (barely) covered crotch. Despite the fact that I had long recovered from the unwilling sexual activity in the limousine and wasn't feeling aroused at all, the fabric was sufficiently sheer and tight to subtly display the shape of the plump soft vaginal lips between my wide-spread legs.

Now realizing what "show time" meant, I started to panic. I frantically pulled and slammed at the restraints holding down my wrists, and tried to kick my feet apart behind me, but in vain.

As I continued to struggle violently against the restraints, the sudden deep male voice was a shock.

"The subject seems to have regained consciousness, on schedule. And she seems to awaken quite noisily."

I heard footsteps, and saw a large man, in the skeletal and muscular sense, enter my field of vision. He was wearing a mask hood. The fact that there was someone now in the room with me was both comforting and, after a little reflection, terrifying.

"Who are you, and where am I?"

There was a silence, as though he was contemplating exactly how to answer, which was even more frightening.

"It does not matter who I am or where you are, and in fact if you knew that, you would never be allowed to leave here," he responded, finally. The voice was deep.

"You are here as part of our mutual agreement to both entertain us, and to be a subject for scientific research."

Fearing the worst, I thought about my next question.

"What kind of entertainment, and what kind of 'scientific research'?"

His next response came with no hesitation.

"We are interested in how much sexual pleasure a young woman can endure. I am sure you can imagine the entertainment possibilities in such an experiment, particularly if there is audience participation."

The last words were chilling. I finally screwed up the courage to ask, fearing the answer, "You said I would not be allowed to leave if I knew who you are. Under what conditions will I be allowed to leave?"

Again without hesitation, he replied, "If you fulfill the agreement, and are cooperative in our research, you will be allowed to leave here unharmed and you will be paid in cash. If you are uncooperative, you will be punished, until you cooperate.

"I will not describe the punishment, but believe me, you will be most unwilling to not cooperate after the slightest taste of our displeasure.

"You know you have a safe phrase if you can't handle it, and you also know that if you use it, the deal is off, and you leave empty handed. Do you remember what it is? You may speak it now to verify without invoking the contract."

I nodded. "It is 'code red.'"

"Very good."

"And I would like to use it now," I continued. "I feel that I was misled about the nature of the agreement."

He paused.

"Well, that would of course be quite disappointing, both to us and our patrons. It would also be a very bad financial decision on your part.

"However, I was told about the discussion in the limousine. While we believe that your fears are quite misplaced, in light of our interest in you and in continuing the arrangement, I'm prepared to increase your compensation by forty percent, to seven thousand dollars, with a contract addendum. You are obviously in no current position to sign it, but in light of its nature, only our signature is required, since your legal terms have not changed."

Strapped down, feet cuffed behind my head, my ass still hanging over the edge of the platform on camera, as he held up the signed paper and showed it to me, I swallowed hard, and thought again about my student loans. It hadn't actually hurt when she had shoved her finger into my ass in the car, and even if it had, that was a lot of money. I couldn't really afford to turn down the initial offer, and this was so much more. Finally, I nodded in agreement.

"Excellent. Now that we've settled that, you must under-stand that, as you've probably already ascertained, you have no control whatsoever over your immediate fate. I heard you testing your restraints, and you have no doubt already found them insurmountable. You are totally under our control."

Realizing that he was right about my lack of control, I hesitantly ventured, "What does 'cooperative' mean? What do you expect from me?"

"We expect very little of you, actually, since there is very little you can do under your constrained circumstances, and soon there will be even less. Since your fate is hence-forth entirely in our hands, you will simply accept what-ever we propose and choose to do to you without question. Per the agreement, we will do nothing to you that would cause permanent physical injury."

I felt another chill at the word "permanent." I didn't recall that in the agreement.

"We aren't going to blindfold you because, as you will literally soon see, the coming events are intended to be an erotic feast for the eyes of our audience, and it is impor-tant to us for you to also view all that is happening to you, for your own necessary helpless sexual arousal.

"We are also not going to gag you, both so you will be able to use your safe phrase if necessary, and because we are in fact very interested in your verbal reports about what you'll be experiencing. So you may and are in fact encouraged to emit normal noises of pleasure and discom-fort under the circumstances, whether mild or extreme, and even to speak to us. You may even attempt to physi-cally resist, if you wish, since we will find it additionally entertaining, and it will be in utter futility for you.

"But we have no interest in hearing complaints, and any actual verbal objection to anything we do or announce that we will do will result in severe punishment. Though you have a safe phrase, words like 'no,' or 'stop' from you have no meaning in this room, other than, functionally, as a request for extreme pain." He paused.

"Though for all we know, perhaps you enjoy that."

He paused again, to allow me to absorb the words, then continued.

"Since you will have absolutely no control from here on, no further instructions are necessary or even useful. The rules are very simple: We will do most of the actual work and you will perform whatever physical exertions we demand of you at the time, without protest.

"Oh, and this is the last time, until we are through with you, that you will be addressed in the second person. Henceforth, though you are always permitted and even encouraged to speak, you will not be directly addressed at all, and will be discussed and referred to only clinically in the third person, as befits a research subject."

As the import of his words – that other than the safe phrase and loss of the money – I was completely powerless to prevent whatever was about to happen to me started to sink into my consciousness, I heard him say not to me, but apparently to someone else, "I believe the subject is now initially prepared. But even if she is not, it is time to open the door and invite in her audience."

Though now thoroughly frightened, I resolved to myself that while I would cooperate by his definition, and earn the money, I would not give them the satisfaction of any discernible pleasure from me.

4

=====

THE BINDING

Still lying on my back on the performance platform, almost naked, wrists strapped down and feet cuffed behind my head, I was frightened of what was soon to come, all the more so because I didn't know what it would be.

But I didn't have long to wait.

A few moments after I heard the instructions to open the door to the theater, someone obeyed them, and people started to wander in, still murmuring from their conversation outside.

"Finally. I hope the show is as good as the last time," I heard one say. All of them were masked, though not with his full hood. Judging from body types, they seemed to be a mix of women and men, but more men.

"Magnificent young creature," remarked one of the latter. "Yes, quite lovely, I'd love to do her myself," came the voice of someone clearly female.

I watched as they slowly took their seats and settled in.

"Good evening, ladies and gentleman. As you can see, we have a spectacular show in store for you tonight."

It was the voice of the large masked man who had given me the brief instructions minutes before, who was apparently the impresario for it.

"Often in such presentations, the audience isn't admitted until the subject is completely prepared for our entertainment, but our entertainment philosophy here is that the preparation is itself a critically important feature of the performance, and for us and even more for her, it is quite elaborate, taking up to or over an hour before the intermission and the main event."

I chilled again at hearing these words, wondering what the "preparation" would entail, what the "main event" was to be, and pulled and kicked at my bonds once again, in continued futility.

"As you can see, while she was sedated earlier and we now have her restrained and fully under our control, we don't consider it adequate for the full effect of the experience we desire for both her and ourselves. To begin the preparation, I'd like to first introduce my lovely and talented assistants. First, Dora."

I bent my head up and watched as the beautiful young voluptuous dark-haired Asian-looking woman entered the room. She was no longer in her chauffeur's uniform. She had apparently slipped into something more comfortable after delivering me (and perhaps undressing and redressing me while I was unconscious and helping to put me in my current restraints). She was wearing only a tight white corset and thigh-height stockings with heels. As she walked in front of me, she stopped and bowed deeply to the audience, the bare breasts above the corset hanging down, while exposing to me all that lay between her lower cheeks.

She was clearly shaven or waxed between her legs, and my eyes widened as I could see both in front of me and in close up on a monitor what appeared to be the flare of a plug emerging from the stretched anus directly above her hairless vulva.

"Now Nora."

As the next woman entered behind the first, I had to assume from the name and her appearance that this was the woman who had examined and then drugged me. She was also out of uniform; she was now bare breasted, similarly attired to the chauffeur, but in red, somewhat matching her auburn hair. Her own deep bow upon her arrival in front of me similarly revealed an absence of pubic hair, and the presence of an anal plug. I now felt sort of even in terms of her having seen my own privates.

"And finally, Esmeralda."

So that was her name. Or at least her stage name. Her blonde hair was undone from when I'd first met her on the street outside the yoga studio, now reaching down to her naked ass. She had apparently exchanged her stuffy conservative business suit for something more engaging. She was now dressed or, rather, barely dressed like the others, except in black. At this point, on her own bow, I wasn't surprised to see her similarly uncoiffed and ass plugged. Each having straightened up after their lascivious bows, the three women then stood briefly in front of me facing the audience, hands behind their backs, as he continued to speak.

"As I noted, the subject is restrained, but not sufficiently for our purposes. You will note that she's continued to struggle against her restraints even after you entered the theater.

"Because we don't want to have to continually fight with her, it is most important psychologically to dramatically increase her feelings of powerlessness and bring her to understand the utter futility of resistance to what we plan for her. So before we do anything else we must first thoroughly end any further struggling."

As he was speaking, the three women had quickly walked around behind me, and two of them had lifted my torso and legs by my cuffed feet and head, rotating me up and forward onto my upper buttocks. I heard a snap as a post was apparently rapidly raised and locked in place vertically behind me by the third woman, and my feet were rested against it behind my head.

"When you entered, the subject could kick and wiggle the feet, move the head around to view her surroundings, and pull and move against her wrist restraints, all of which activities are needless distractions from the inevitable upcoming events."

One of the women behind me – Dora or Nora – had already crossed and firmly held my feet over each other, while I could feel the other expertly and rapidly wrapping and cinching soft rope around them, binding them tightly both together and to the upright post behind me.

As this was occurring, having apparently lifted the post for them, Esmeralda had moved quickly back around to the front, where she was already starting to tighten my wrist restraints on both sides. I could hear the clicking of ratchets as she silently cranked each side, each click binding my hands more firmly and immovably to the platform.

"In addition to immobilizing the subject and removing the distractions of the muscles of the limbs, you can see that we have put her in a better posture both for her to observe the events in which she is to be the star performer, and to provide more ready access to and a better angle at our new precious now-defenseless commodities between the wide-spread legs, the latter of which are now useless to anyone, including her, other than for our own visual enjoyment."

As what seemed to be stage patter continued, the already unreleasable restraints on my wrists were now tightly cinched at my sides against the platform. As a result of this, my arms were pressed against the back of my upper thighs, just below (or what would be below if they were in a normal posture) my hips, to the point that I could get no motion from them at all regardless of how I strained at them.

This had all happened within the span of a minute or two. I don't know if, even had I understood what was about to happen to me, I could have even fought to prevent it, but it had happened so rapidly that the situation had quickly become completely hopeless.

"The subject is now thoroughly under control, unable any longer to struggle against her bindings, and we have almost completed the initial immobilization. All that we need do now is to restrain the head so she can't move it, and strap the ass with its warm tight holes down to the performance platform, so that it won't move when we take our pleasure with them."

I watched on the monitors, in a bizarre combination of fright and fascination, as one of the women who had just so firmly bound my feet together held my head in place as the other silently lowered a padded rectangular frame over the upper part of it. She tightened it up against my temples and forehead, and then rigidly attached it to the pole behind me just above my bound feet. It wasn't painfully tight, but it too was firm, a stiff band preventing any motion of my head. Now I could only look forward, within the range of the motion of my eyes, at the audience and the monitors above them.

As my field of vision was being thus restricted, I watched on one of the monitors as Esmeralda pulled up something like a seat belt from the platform next to my left hip, and threaded it between my upward-pointing thighs and waist. She then clicked it in on the other side, next to my right hip, and wordlessly cinched it tight, forcing my lower body down even further. The strength of the strap enhancing the 124 pounds of my weight on them, my upper buttocks were now firmly flattened to the platform, and essentially glued in place on it by the static friction.

The spread crevice between my legs, in the middle of which my most intimate bodily parts resided under the sheer panties, including the lower one whose violation I so feared, was aimed forward, and slightly overhung the end of the platform, apparently with nothing below to obstruct access to it.

"The subject is now realizing her total inability to resist us. The normal sense of control over her own destiny has been fully drained from her, replaced by feelings of futility and fear, perhaps even terror, as we've now assumed full ownership of the creature.

"None of the external muscles are any longer of any utility to her. The goal of this initial exercise is to shift her mental focus from the distractions of those usual muscles she uses – in the calves, the thighs, the arms, the neck – to only those internal to the body. That is, the only muscles over which the creature now has any useful control are those involved in the most emotionally intense exertions of all, those of sex and other natural mammalian bodily functions.

"Though the creature's torso is now locked firmly in place, and she cannot move the limbs, or head, she can still open and close and move her eyes, and control her upper lips and tongue, to report her sensations to us.

"She also continues to fully control the abdominal muscles, pelvic floor, and bladder, including the cylindrical and circular muscular structures in our new tight cunt and anal sphincter between the thighs currently, but only for the moment, hidden from our eager eyes.

"Once those are unveiled and exposed, unable to engage in any other activities, all of her attention will henceforth be focused on using them to visually and physically entertain and pleasure us, and they will get a workout presently as they've never had before."

He was right; I'd never felt so powerless in my life.

Staring straight ahead, I was unable to move anything other than my eyes and facial muscles, able only to wiggle my fingers and toes. Of major muscles, I could only squeeze my internals which, as he said, were now clenched in fright verging on terror at his emotionless clinical description of both my current helpless situation, and the immediate future of the sensitive orifices between my legs, particularly the one directly below my vagina, whose violation I had for so long dreaded.

And not only was I to be discussed only in the third person, as he had warned before the show began, but I now realized that his crude descriptions of my body parts would be impersonal as well. My limbs were "the" limbs. My head was "the" head. I wasn't even a person at all; I was merely an animal, a "creature," a bound pet utterly possessed by them for their pleasure.

Worse, my vagina wasn't even "her vagina," but *their* "cunt," as though as it was no longer my own. I now felt like nothing so much as a motionless warm sex robot for them, with clutching holes but no agency, as apparently I was about to inevitably become.

But I didn't know that it was soon to get even worse.

5

=====

THE UNVEILING

When I had first regained consciousness, I had been restrained, but I was now completely immobilized, and totally powerless to prevent anything from happening to any part of my body, not least those parts between my legs, protruding unobstructed past the edge of the performance platform, and currently protected only by a flimsy sheer garment.

It wasn't a theoretical fear; he was strongly implying that I was soon to be helplessly sexually exploited, in ways I couldn't presently contemplate, repeatedly, including the anal penetration from which I had foolishly thought I'd exempted myself. And the only way to prevent it was to bail out with my safe phrase, and no compensation.

As he continued to accurately describe my fear and, frighteningly, his plans for my immediate future over which I had no control, the two women at my sides each reached behind my clamped head, parted my long brown tresses, and draped half of them over the front of each of my shoulders.

I could do nothing as they then gently excavated my (unfortunately, in the current circumstances, ample) breasts from in between and under my arms, and brought them forward to prominence, raising and massaging them briefly under the sheer bikini top.

At the touch of their gentle expert warm hands and fingers on the sensitive skin surrounding my nipples, my fear was quickly becoming alloyed with unwanted pleasure.

After a minute or two of this mammary stimulation, one of them picked up a pair of shears, and carefully snipped the top in between them, freeing it from them, as the other woman pulled the scanty garment completely out from behind me. Now, as things continued to grow worse with each event, my naked bosom with its swelling nipples was on full display to the crowd and cameras.

On one of the monitors above the audience (which, with my head now locked in place, I suddenly realized must be primarily for the benefit of my eyes) I could see, even as I could feel each woman start to gently stroke and squeeze the exposed little mounds in the middle of my large aureoles with their fingers.

To my shock and dismay, as they had in the limousine, the tender nubs almost instantly started to further swell in response to the new undesired stimulation.

The audience murmured quietly.

"Such a gorgeous presentation," I heard a woman admire. Despite my fear, head immobilized but rolling my eyes up to see myself on the video screen, I had to admit that, if I could somehow detach myself from the fact that it was happening to *me*, it was a very erotic sight.

The man gave a slight nod to the two women on each side of me, and clearly this was rehearsed, because they each leaned in, cupped and lifted a breast. After weighing them in one hand as they rubbed and squeezed the swollen nipples some more with the other, they each took a whole aureole on each side into their mouth.

Now they started to suck in and flick their tongues over the center of both of my naked breasts, already somewhat swollen from the manipulation of the nipples and hardening more with the new ministrations of their lips and tongues.

I gasped at the sudden sensuous sensation, and the gasp grew involuntarily into a moan, so quickly had my earlier resolve to show no emotion dissolved. I had had my breasts and nipples sucked, but never by a woman, and never both at once. The new experience combined with my utterly powerless circumstances was unexpectedly powerfully arousing to me.

"The initial psychological preparation is already starting to take effect," he remarked, almost casually, "as you can see by the growing stain between the spread thighs."

One of the cameras slowly zoomed in on my crotch, and I was now mortified to see in the monitor the so-rapid betrayal of my body, as my seeping vaginal secretions were indeed starting to dampen the thin material of the tight garment through which I, along with the audience, could also clearly see the outlines of my now-swelling labia in high resolution. As the camera zoomed, some of the attendees were looking directly at me, but many in the back seemed to be looking up and past me; there must have been monitors behind me to similarly display to them, in close up, my ongoing humiliation.

"This doesn't necessarily mean that the creature is joyfully anticipating her upcoming ordeal, of course. Even in fear, it is a natural reaction; some evolutionary psychologists believe that this lubrication would simply be a normal autonomic response of a woman's cunt to the potential prospect that it is about to be forcibly penetrated.

"It would be a useful adaptation to reduce the level of injury during rape, which would have been a very common occurrence throughout most of human history.

"So she shouldn't be embarrassed that she appears to be eager for fucking, under the circumstances currently beyond her control."

The words partially explained my seemingly shameful lack of will but, to my further shame, what came next was worse, as indeed each progressive event had been so far.

I felt him effortlessly separate the tight fabric from my groin with his right hand, and insert two fingers of his other one underneath it into my clenched but now-defenseless moistening vagina.

"Yes, we could see it from the dampened panties. But I can also feel the juices of lust now seeping from our hungry cunt. She will be a most excellent subject, I believe."

He removed the fingers and walked to the front row, allowing each person seated there to smell them. Each sniffed and nodded, as though approving a bottle of fine wine just brought to the table while dining. He then walked back to the platform, again pulled the material away from me, and dipped them again into the warm wet opening between my legs, apparently for fresh secretions. This time he held them up to my own immobilized face.

"There are pheromones in cunt juices that increase a woman's desire when detected by olfactory organs, even when they are her own," he explained, not to me but to the audience.

"The women in the front row were probably turned on by the scent, and perhaps the men as well." Some in the audience nodded in appreciation and agreement.

As the two women at my sides continued to gently mouth my breasts, he covered my own mouth with his right hand, carefully to prevent any opportunity for me to bite it. I now had no access to life-giving air except through my nostrils, and he held the soiled fingers right below them.

"We will now give the subject several whiffs of her own musk, to help her prepare to succumb to her deep-felt desires to pleasure both us and herself, which she had previously been unaware even existed."

I had smelled my own secretions in the past, of course, out of curiosity. But the sensation of being forced to do so, as I deeply breathed in their strong scent, combined with my helpless situation as the two women continued to gently tug and suckle at my nipples with their soft warm mouths, my bared breasts rising and falling with each deep aromatic inhalation and release, was emotionally overwhelming. I could now clearly feel the blood flowing to my groin with my unwelcome excitement, and see the continuing swelling of my now-sensitive labia and clitoris against the tight sheer fabric, as my tightly bound body subconsciously continued to betray my conscious desires.

"And with that, I believe that it is time for the unveiling, and continuing the preparation for the main event."

With the words, he lowered the fingers and removed the hand from my mouth, then picked up the shears that had earlier cut the top covering my now-bared breasts.

I watched the close-up of my snatch still on the monitor in fascinated mortification as he carefully, almost ceremonially lifted and snipped the right side of the sheer garment above my swollen genitals, and gently pulled it aside and set it down on the platform next to my right hip.

He then did the same with the left side by my left hip.
The newly liberated center section still covering my most
private region seemed to defy gravity, apparently slightly
glued in place against my spread damp engorged vulva by
the moisture continuing to seep from my now fully
aroused vagina.

He slowly pulled it away, gently brushing the free end of
it up and down against my swollen clitoris and outer vaginal lips as my breasts continued to be suckled, sending
unwanted but sublime little shivers of desire up my spine.

This went on for almost a minute, and another of what I
feared were to be many unbidden moans of sexual pleasure to come escaped my lips.

He finally ended the genital stimulation with the soft
fabric, and dropped the piece down to hang over the edge
of the platform below my cleft, fully displaying to the
crowd and cameras, one of which had remained zoomed in
on it in high resolution, that which the women had been
admiring in the limousine – my spread, wet, engorged
vulva, and the wrinkled circular pucker of my tender anus
below it. The latter was clenching tightly with my still-
growing fear, and glistening with the vaginal secretions of
my excitement, now not merely seeping, but fully dripping
down on it from over my perineum above.

And to my shock, I could see why I had felt strangely different beneath the panties when I had first regained consciousness; like the other women, all between my legs was
now completely devoid of hair.

There was a gasp of pleasure at the new erotic sight
from the audience. "Such a beautiful naked wet swollen
pussy and ass hole," a woman in the front row remarked.
"She must wax."

"For those wondering," he explained, hearing the words and other murmurs, "the creature was shorn, and bathed and cleansed in all aspects except one, as part of the pre-show preparation. We believe it makes for a more aesthetically pleasing presentation.

"In addition," he went on, as he gently brushed the backs of his finger tips against my now-hairless and defenseless labia, "it considerably enhances the sensitivity of our new pussy to licking or fucking, both of which it will be abundantly experiencing over the next few hours."

The so-very slight stroking of my newly-bald and now fully swollen genitals was an amazing sensation that I'd never experienced before, and it sent more shivers up my spine and elicited another moan from me.

But I was now not just frightened, but angry. Other than trimming my bikini line, I'd had that hair since puberty, and had considered it a badge of adulthood, albeit a private one, at least until now. Even in the context of all else that was happening to me, it seemed like a terrible violation of my person. I felt as though it was a breach of the agreement, but it wasn't exactly an injury, nor was it permanent; it would grow back if I allowed it to.

I was also curious and not a little concerned about what he meant by "cleansed in all aspects except one," but he didn't elaborate. I had never felt so totally exposed, a feeling accentuated by the next crude words I heard from the admiring audience.

"I would love to stuff my cock into those soft warm holes," one of the men enthused. "Look," replied another, "see how the cunt juices are still dripping down over that tight ass hole. With all that lubrication, I think I could shove it in there right now."

The last words were truly frightening, because the one time I had attempted anal sex, under pressure from the erstwhile boyfriend, the pain had been terrible. I thought of my safe phrase, but also remembered the consequences of using it.

The crowd was allowed to simply take in the now amazingly erotic view for a minute or two, as he carefully lifted first my right buttock from behind, and then my left, gently tugging the cut garment from underneath my belted weight, finally pulling it through my cleft and out from behind, and disposing of it.

With the panties – the last pathetic defense of my private parts – totally removed, I was now as naked as I'd ever been in my life, while completely immobilized, defenseless to whatever any of them wanted to do with what lay between my helplessly spread and bound legs.

I saw that some of the men in front of me had actually released their growing members from their pants and were stroking them, perhaps in eager anticipation of soon stuffing them deeply into me against my will. A couple women had their hands buried in their own crotches as well and were rubbing them, apparently themselves aroused at the sight of my humiliatingly exposed completely shorn vulnerable holes, perhaps imagining themselves in my mortified powerless circumstances.

"As I said, I believed we would have a magnificent specimen," he announced in a pleased tone, "but even I am astonished at the beauty of what lies between the soft, tender thighs. Observe not just the dripping of our new cunt, but also how our pussy lips and clit are already fully engorged, swollen and eager. But just to fully demonstrate to the creature that this naked pussy now belongs to us..."

I gasped in surprise as I felt his hard and apparently thick penis suddenly rush into my defenseless vagina – now well lubricated with my own growing involuntary passion – wide, deep, and full.

"Ah, we indeed have acquired a warm soft cunt that feels even more delicious than it looks," he proclaimed.

He slid his member slowly out and then back in and, again unbid, another moan of pleasure escaped my lips. Both of my hardened nipples continuing to be enveloped in the soft warm suckling mouths, my tingling cylinder stretched wide by the engorged stiff shaft, I involuntarily squeezed at the new sensation of a hairless copulation of my vulva, swollen and firm with blood, and now sublimely sensitive.

He continued to speak to the audience even as he continued his now-intoxicating, leisurely thrusts in and out of me as, eyes closed, I softly, helplessly grunted with pleasure from each deep stretching stroke of the thick meat.

"Our new tight twat is clutching my own swollen and hardened cock most eagerly now. This is a perfect example of how when all other muscles are unavailable to the creature, and she is undistracted by them, the only ones that are being used get her full attention.

"But while we will try to keep our juicy, hungry young pussy occupied, that is not the primary object of tonight's entertainment."

After only a minute or so of intensely pleasurable slow stroking in and out, with the last words, he completely withdrew the thick piston from my now-ravenous upper orifice, leaving it suddenly feeling barren and clutching, opening and closing in frustration at the sudden absence.

It also left me now perversely desperate for more of the intensely pleasurable deep thrusting in and out of it, despite my continuing anger and fright at my powerless situation.

But my stomach was also knotting as I heard the words, fearing very much what might come next, in light of what Esmeralda had told me in the limousine. My vagina empty, with his *next* words, my deep dread was immediately borne out.

"No, tonight, we are going to make our beautiful little lower flower blossom for our mutual pleasure."

As he was speaking them, he inserted his right index finger through my tightly clenched but ultimately helpless anal sphincter, now slick from the lubricating juices continuing to seep and drip from the fully aroused and still-open entrance above it. I felt the muscular ring stretch uncomfortably from the first knuckle passing through it as he sunk the digit deep into my rectum.

I jumped, albeit only internally, given my rigid bondage, at the unwelcome intrusion and spoke my first words since the entrance of the crowd and the beginning of the ordeal. In my fright, forgetting his earlier warning, I moaned without thinking.

"No. Please, not there."

6

THE PUNISHMENT

Completely frozen by my taut bonds, as I futilely protested the finger stretching my helpless anus, he looked directly at my face, for the first time since the audience had entered.

I could almost sense an angry glare under his mask at what he must have thought was my impudence, about which I had been warned before the "performance" had begun. The women who had been suckling at my breasts could apparently sense it as well, and raised their heads from them, silently backing away from my sides.

He calmly and slowly slid the intruding finger of his right hand from my lower hole, then suddenly, with the open palm of it, started to harshly slap the shorn flesh and the orifices between my legs, still tingling with pleasure from the previous stroking of his penis. Each sharp blow elicited a yelp of pain from me but also, to my continuing dismay, it seemed to further engorge the stinging and swollen lips and clitoris with blood and arousal.

I considered using my safe phrase but, perversely, my desire started to increase with every strike as well, to the point that I was actually, and shockingly to me, approaching an orgasm, and now hopefully anticipating it despite the pain. But then, as abruptly as he'd started, he stopped slapping me between my wide-spread thighs.

On the verge of my climax, I couldn't tell whether the intended punishment had been the blows to my genitals, or their sudden cessation, with the new urgent unsatisfied sexual hunger now flooding my groin.

Either way, I hoped the punishment was over, but then I helplessly watched as he dipped the first two fingers of his left hand into my now even-wetter vagina as he had before, swirling and collecting the secretions on them.

Then, using the fresh vaginal fluid as a lubricant, he inserted the left index finger through my sphincter into my lower colon, much deeper than the previous right one had been, as far in as it could go. He wiggled and rotated it slowly around inside me, as I remained silent in both fright and now a strange lust despite the unfamiliar discomfort of it. He then slowly slid it out, and did the same with the middle finger on the same hand, which was even longer.

After a few more seconds of thus stirring my rectum with his fingers, he slowly withdrew the third finger, and lifted both of the now-aromatic digits on his left hand up to my face. Then he slowly and deliberately and unavoidably jammed them into my immovable nostrils, now flared wide in terror.

With the same open right palm with which he had previously tortured my shorn vulva and anus, without warning, he suddenly sharply slapped first my right cheek, and then my left, as he held me by the nose with the defiled fingers. After gasping at the initial shock, I could feel the sting on both sides, and see the rush of blood to my reddening flesh in the closeup of my face in a monitor.

He removed the fingers but continued to hold them just below my nose. He once again covered my mouth with the other hand.

This time, instead of just my vaginal secretions, I was forced to smell again those vaginal juices that had been used for my anal lubrication, combined now with the stink from the interior of my rectum, as my spread bare genitals continued to deeply throb with unwanted desire.

As I tried to calmly breathe deeply in and out despite my weird mix of simultaneous fright and arousal, and the sharp odor, he finally announced, "I must apologize for the interruption, ladies and gentleman. Apparently, the creature has already forgotten her instructions. She was to report to us on her sensations, but she was given to understand, or so I thought, that we have no interest in her protestations, under threat of harsh punishment if she expresses them regardless."

After a minute or so, he removed the fingers from beneath my nostrils and the hand from my mouth. He reached behind my head with both hands.

My feet had been crossed before they were bound, and the soles were pointing sideways in opposite directions: right pointing left, and left pointing right. He started to gently tickle them with his fingers. I couldn't even wiggle them to escape.

My giggles were involuntary and genuine. But he continued, with more intensity, and I started to feel terrified as the initial giggles turned into screams of laughter from the now-torturous sensations, to the point that my abdomen was starting to become exhausted from it as my other muscles remained constrained by my tight bindings. I was internally begging for the tickling to stop but not daring to voice it under the circumstances.

Just as I thought I could take no more, on the verge of using the safe phrase, it did suddenly stop.

He then picked up a light rod, and started to tap it gently, rhythmically, against the sole of my left foot, behind my right ear. I didn't know what was to come next, but after several seconds of the gentle tapping he swatted it hard against the center without warning, and I involuntarily shrieked from the sudden unexpected sharp pain.

"The soles of the feet and particularly the arch are surprisingly sensitive," he explained to the audience. "The beating of them is in fact an established centuries-old torture technique, most popularly known as 'bastinado.' If done correctly, it is one of several means of inflicting severe pain without causing actual injury."

As he related the history, he had started tapping the other sole, and fear started to well up in my gut, still aching from the brutality of the forced laughter. I now knew what was coming, but I didn't know when, though I hoped that my new resolve to show no emotion at the now-expected pain would hold better than my previous one to show no pleasure. I thought again about the safe phrase, but I also thought about the money.

The tapping continued and then I suddenly felt the searing agony of the next strike, harder than the first. I maintained silence this time, though just barely. But I couldn't avoid a grimace, as I could feel my eyes moistening with the beginning of tears.

"Well, the creature took that one more stoically. That's a good sign, despite previous evidence, that she is in fact trainable.

"As I noted, it is a torture technique, but we are not about either sadism, or masochism or pain at all here. In fact, I do not enjoy inflicting pain. For me, this is all about intense forced sexual pleasure.

"But when there is disobedience, punishment must be sure and swift, or the insubordination will only continue and grow worse. I'd like to trust that the creature now truly understands the consequences of disregarding our conditions for her ultimate release."

Even though he didn't use the word "you," I knew that he was really addressing me, not the audience. Upon hearing the words, I tried to focus, and concentrate on not allowing any further objections to escape my lips. I now realized that, despite my long-seated fear of it, the punishment for doing so could very easily be much worse than anal penetration. The latter might hurt, but it wouldn't be a "permanent" injury, and if I had to resort to the safe phrase, there was now seven thousand dollars at stake.

"But to be certain, I am going to have to momentarily break show protocol, and directly address the subject."

With the words, he looked again into my eyes and then, still staring, reached down, and slowly inserted three fingers of his right hand deep into my defenseless vagina.

"Tell me *now*, whose tight cunt are my fingers filling?"

I stared back for a moment, confused, and then replied, unthinking, "They're in my vagina."

Upon hearing the words, now stroking the fingers in and out of me, he reached up and suddenly slapped the right cheek of my immobilized face with his left palm, as he had with his right when the punishment had started.

"Tell me *whose* cunt this is!"

Cheek reddening and stinging again, now I understood. Fully aware of the audience watching and listening, and continuing to be mortified beyond imagining in my spread nakedness, I quietly responded as I now knew he wanted.

"It's *your* cunt."

He nodded in approval. Then he removed the fingers from my vagina, and I watched and felt him force his thick thumb into my slick tight anal passage just below it.

"Now, whose *ass hole* is this?"

I winced at the sudden stretch of my sphincter as the wider knuckle passed through it.

"It's *your* ass hole." I hesitated, and then continued.

"To do with what you will."

He smiled, the first time I'd ever seen it. "Good girl."

He pulled the thumb in my rectum back through my clenching anus, and turned back to the audience.

"As I said," he continued, gently cleaning my nostrils, and then his soiled fingers with a warm damp cloth, "tonight's performance is about anal play, made apparently all the more entertaining by the creature's seeming fear of it. Thus, it will be our goal tonight to train her to not only end her needless trepidation of it, but instead to start to actively lust for it, even after she has departed our presence and gone back to her now-enlightened life. She may or may not be interested in such training but, as she has already been told, her interests are of no moment to us."

He paused, apparently for dramatic effect, to shift the subject back to the immediate issue.

"Now that our new tight warm holes are fully exposed and totally available to us, and she finally understands the rules, the next step is to slowly get our new lower orifice used to penetration, to train and open it for us to all enjoy its use, as I was starting to do before she so rudely interrupted the performance with her pointless whining."

7

THE INITIAL INSERTION

The cruel punishment seemed to be over but, my face, genitals, and soles still stinging from the slaps and swats, and abdomen still sore from the tickling, I remained completely immobilized. My thighs were still spread wide and the naked hairless holes between them totally vulnerable, and I was still utterly powerless to prevent whatever was to happen to them next. As when the audience had first entered, I again didn't have to wait long.

"Esmeralda, please bring me the first training device."

Upon hearing the request, apparently also realizing that the punishment was over, the two women who had abandoned my breasts when it had begun returned to them, and once again took my swollen nubs into their seemingly hungry soft warm mouths. In response to it, Esmeralda came to him bearing a strange-looking object, which he took from her and held up in front of me so I could see it as I could feel my nipples being gently suckled again, but he faced the audience. A camera zoomed in on it. It was gray, a few inches long, not wide, but slightly wider on the two ends, with a narrower neck in the middle. It had two rubber bulbs attached and what appeared to be a metallic collar at one end, and a little opening in the other.

"Note that this is narrow at one end, and tapered and not currently wide at all, so it will slip easily and even painlessly into what is now our ass hole, even if she resists. In her current circumstances, she's not going anywhere, the ass isn't going anywhere, and the tight sphincter in the middle of it is an immovable object, or at least the center of it is. And against it, this well-lubricated device with my hand behind it will be the proverbial irresistible force.

"When I center it on the now-slickened lower hole and push on it, it will have nowhere to go except to slide deep into the egress of the helpless ass. The only current freedom of movement for the tight, clenching lower hole is in its diameter, which as part of the preparation we will ultimately properly enlarge for both our and her pleasure."

As he was speaking, he had dipped his hand into a jar of lubricant, and was slowly but thoroughly slathering it onto what was apparently the tapered business end of the device. I watched, perversely fascinated, trying to imagine the sensation of it sliding through a tender orifice that had heretofore been used only for exits, and also frightened at the realization that I would very soon experience it and that there was nothing I could do to prevent it.

"Once inserted deep into our tight warm ass hole, through the tense circular muscular ring, resisting in futility, it will then be expanded within the creature."

He gave a couple of pumps with one of the bulbs to demonstrate how it would so very soon uncontrollably and hugely swell inside my bottom.

"We will make the device far too large for her to expel, even with the abundant lubrication and the few muscles available to her, at least not without severe pain to our anal ring that she seems so much to fear."

He released a valve, and it shrunk once again.

I watched a close up in the monitor as he then reentered my vagina with three of his now well-lubricated fingers, tenderly rubbing my engorged clitoris with the thumb of the same hand, and slowly spreading the fingers to gently stretch and fuck me with them, as the nurse had earlier in the limousine, as my breasts continued to be suckled.

I moaned again as I realized that, even with the fear gripping my internals, rather than ending my sexual excitement as I would have thought, the recent punishment and prospective violation of both of my private holes had if anything accentuated it, and my genitals, with the few body muscles available to me, were more swollen, sensitive, and eager than ever.

After a minute or so of fingering and thus pleasuring my vagina, he took the device in his other hand, and I could watch and feel him touch the end of it against the sensitive center of the entrance to my bowels below it. I shuddered in fear as well as I could in my tight restraints as he then slowly pushed it in a bit, then pulled it out, then in and out, several times. In my continuing fright, despite the tingling pleasure of the massage of my vulva and stretching of my vagina, trembling, I used every available muscle to try to force it back each time. But, as he had said, I had no power whatsoever to prevent either its entrance or exit as it slid back and forth through my anal passage.

"Note that the creature is clenching and straining, trying to prevent the entrance and even to push it out of our tight young ass hole," he clinically observed, as he continued to gently and seemingly effortlessly stroke it in and out of me. "She may resist if she wishes; she won't be punished for it as long as she doesn't verbally object.

"One purpose of this exercise, among others, is in fact to continue to break down her resistance, both by demonstrating to her the utter futility of it, and by persuading her to accept the most intense sensual adventure that she is being offered by us, likely far beyond anything in her experience, with a hint of the potential pleasure to come."

As he was speaking the last few words, he had removed it, allowing my open sphincter to close again momentarily, but he kept it gently pressed against the tightly clenched exit that was slowly, despite my futile resistance, becoming an unwilling but powerlessly resisting entrance.

"As I said, the strength of my arm far exceeds that of our tight anal ring, particularly since she is untrained and doesn't properly exercise it."

And with those words, continuing to massage my genitals, he slid it back in again, and then relentlessly kept sliding it in, sinking it into and burying it deep in my rectum, as he had described. I issued a little grunt at the unfamiliar and uncomfortable sensation of being forced open from the outside, against which I was totally powerless, but was surprised that in fact it didn't actually hurt and, in combination with the other sensations, it even felt a little exciting, also creating a new unfamiliar sensual pleasure.

"It is fully in now," he announced.

"If I were to let go of it, the subject could still force it out using the normal abdominal muscles for expelling things from an ass, and in fact I can feel her attempting to do so even now in utter futility, but once we expand it sufficiently, it will not be coming out and I'll no longer need to hold it in our ass hole against the creature's will.

"Esmeralda, it's time to start enlarging it inside her."

He was right; still frightened and now desperate, I was experimentally internally straining to try to push it out against his hand, as though I was relieving myself, before it could be expanded within me, but to no avail. Expressionless, Esmeralda silently started to pump one of the bulbs as he continued to hold the device firmly and deep in my bottom while continuing to finger and stretch my vagina above it.

"The creature is starting to feel the inner plug swell at the exit of the intestines, filling the rectum. She is probably feeling like she needs to shit, particularly if she isn't used to this sort of thing."

I could, as he said, feel it growing inside me with each little squeeze of the woman's hand, the strange yet somehow familiar pressure making me indeed feel like I needed to go. In my otherwise decisionless circumstances, I decided to volunteer the first words I had spoken since the harsh punishment.

"Yes, that is how it feels. It's quite unpleasant."

"Interesting that the creature is finally cooperating; perhaps the brief but necessary punishment has clarified her mind," he noted to the audience. "Well, unpleasant or not, she has no choice in the matter. Perhaps she'll inform us when she gets more used to it."

After another minute or so, it felt like it was filling me beyond the capacity of my colon, but then it seemed to stop getting bigger.

"I believe that the inner plug is now fully expanded," he observed.

"That will be all for now here, Esmeralda. Time to go get her initial treatment."

With his words, I could now clearly feel that the device had become far too large for me to expel it through my anal sphincter, and my ongoing sense of utter helplessness in my situation had continued to grow along with it. His other hand free now that he no longer had to use it to hold the object in me against the continuing futile force of my internal muscles, he shifted it to the other bulb as he continued to finger fuck my exposed vagina.

"Now that the device is unremovably inside the subject, I am inflating the outer part of it, to prevent her from swallowing it *into* the ass. So she is also going to start feeling the pressure of it against the exit from the outside.

"As both ends expand, the neck in the center also grows somewhat, starting for the first time, but not last, to forcibly stretch the muscles of our warm young anal ring and begin widening it, a process ultimately necessary for both us and her to properly enjoy its use. As I do so, my continuing pleasuring of our cunt and clit both excites her and helps our tightly clenched but slowly stretching sphincter below them to relax for us to soon use it."

He was again describing exactly what I was feeling, as I was at the same time wondering with no little trepidation what the "initial treatment" would be that he had sent Esmeralda to fetch.

"It stings a little, but it's getting a little better with time, and the finger fucking actually feels very good."

"An excellent report," he declared, as he continued to expand the outside of the device, putting new pressure against the entrance of my widening anal sphincter as he continued to stroke and stretch my vagina above with his fingers. Both actions were generating more and more pleasure in the tingling holes between my wide-spread thighs.

"It will continue to get easier for her. You may recall I noted when she was unveiled that, prior to the performance, the subject had been cleansed in all aspects except one. Since we only just acquired her, we can't know when the creature's bowels were last evacuated, but it doesn't matter, because we are going to help her do it presently, to continue her preparation and provide a clear and clean path for our mutual pleasure."

Shocked at the words, I desperately reported, "I don't know what time it is now, but I went just before yoga," irrationally embarrassed at the confession of being human before all these strangers, but hoping beyond hope to avoid whatever he planned without actually verbally objecting, the consequences of which I now understood. But as with all else so far, it was to no avail.

"That is a vaguely interesting report, I suppose," he responded, as he continued to massage my genitals, which were steadily becoming more and more aroused, "but we recently demonstrated to the creature's own nose just how unhygienic she currently is down there. So, as we're going to clean out our new toy regardless, and there's absolutely nothing she can do to prevent it, it's simply too much information."

He had stopped pumping. "Esmeralda, I believe we now have the subject well and securely sealed and ready for her first treatment. Please bring it in."

My eyes widened as the beautiful but still-expressionless woman who had supervised my abduction, later silently and tightly cinched my hands, and had just expanded the device inside me, now appeared in front of my immobilized face trundling a wheeled stand with a large bulging red rubber bag hanging from it, a hose dangling beneath.

"Though the device is indeed starting to stretch and train our new anal sphincter, what I didn't mention is that it also has a tube running through the center of it to provide an open path from the outside to her insides. It is now time to attach the hose of this bag to the well-designed nozzle we have securely embedded into our taut and now-sealed ass hole. Then we will start to fill the creature's lower intestines with its abundant contents, in order to cleanse them with a deep and ample enema.

"This will begin a process that will ultimately provide us with a clean, clutching, lubricated lower orifice, which we will then helplessly stretch wide as we pleasurably stroke our hard thick cocks in and out of it, stuffing our new hungry tight ass with our warm firm meat, and ultimately filling it with our cum."

8

=====

THE FILLING

Even ignoring the crude description of the upcoming fate of my virgin sphincter, the words were shocking.

"Oh god no, not an enema!"

The pain in my feet and cheeks from my recent punishment now almost dissipated but still fresh in my mind, this time I was careful not to say the horrified thought aloud. My only experiences with one had been with a narrow tube and bulb as a constipated child.

My blood ran cold at the apparent size of the bag, and my now utter inability to prevent it from being attached to the large nozzle unremovably stretching and sealing my tender anus, and then filling my bowels from the wrong direction, perhaps beyond their capacity and my endurance. Every step of the "preparation" was continuing to grow worse and worse.

He continued to lecture, as he also continued to gently and pleasantly rub and finger fuck me.

"Note that the device has a quick disconnect for the hose of the bag. Well inflated both at the entrance of our ass hole and inside the rectum, with its swollen lubricated neck between helplessly stretching and widening our tight and still-unwilling sphincter, we now have a perfect seal with which to slowly fill her, with no fear of leakage, or her escaping the needed cleansing."

As he spoke and massaged my genitals, and I continued to be unable to even struggle against it, let alone stop them, I heard a click and felt a little tug from the swollen device embedded in my now-stretched sensitive sphincter.

With the sensation and sound, I realized that, as he had been speaking, Esmeralda had silently and without hesitation attached the hose of the huge bag she had just delivered without my request, and it was now primed to deliver its bulging contents deep into my intestines. Though my heart was now pounding, and I still couldn't quite believe that this was actually happening to me, I was surprised again that, combined with the continuing genital massage, it also provided a little unfamiliar new tingle of pleasure.

He went on with his cold – almost clinical, except for the crude anatomical words – description of the previously unimaginable process I was now about to unwillingly undergo between my thighs and in my abdomen.

"The height of the bag above our immobilized ass hole determines the pressure and rate with which the fluid flows into her helpless bowels. There is a check valve to prevent her from using her internal muscles, the only ones currently available to her, to force it back up the hose through the tube now tightly embedded in the lower hole, but once the bag is empty and she has been properly filled, we will disconnect it to safely and completely seal her up."

As he spoke, the woman lowered the bulging bag of liquid to just a couple feet above the tube stuck in and stretching my sphincter, right in front of me and about level with my terrified eyes. I could also see what appeared to be a small flow meter on the hose through which my lower intestines were about to be helplessly engorged, though it currently was motionless.

"Before we commence the flow into the creature, we want to prepare to distract her from the experience. Esmeralda, please assume the position at our new pussy."

With those words, he backed away, apparently ending the long genital hand massage, at least for the moment. The woman who had just emotionlessly delivered and attached the dreaded full rubber bag to the device help-lessly widening my stretched anus, and who at this point seemed emotionally capable of almost anything, silently approached the platform, and dropped a hinged padded bench down in the front that had apparently been folded within it.

She climbed onto it on her knees, with her own bare hairless plugged anus, and vulva now facing the audience. Her face was just above the enlarged enema nozzle stick-ing out of my own sphincter. She was so close to it that her chin pushed it slightly downward, creating an interesting pressure on it that I could feel down there with the grow-ing sensitivity of my now-taut widened anal ring.

"Very good, my dear. Now, though you have been so instrumental in competently rendering the creature com-pletely powerless to prevent you from starting to fill her, and swell and cleanse the bowels for us, as you do so, par-tially or perhaps even fully compensate her by pleasuring our swollen pussy with your lips and tongue, as only a woman knows how to do to another woman."

Though shocked at the words, I was even more shocked, and moaned in pleasure as she immediately obe-diently placed her warm mouth on my still-swollen defenseless shorn lower lips. My legs still spread wide and held back by the tight bonds on my wrists and feet, I could feel her soft warm lips and tongue go quickly to work.

As she softly licked and sucked at my genitals, the other two women continued to tenderly suckle at my swollen tingling nipples. The sudden contrast between her cold indifference to my bondage and almost torture in which she was a willing, even eager participant, and the gentle lingual and labial love with which her tongue and soft upper lips now greeted my lower ones, was quite jarring.

In the crevice between my helplessly spread thighs, they sweetly sucked at my sensitive bald but now-empty genitals as the tongue swirled my clitoris. I had never received cunnilingus from a woman and, combined with the double breast suckling, had never felt such comprehensive physical pleasure in general, so I didn't really miss the now seemingly trivial fingers in my empty vagina.

But I also started to sense the warm liquid flowing a few moments after another audible click indicated that, as she had started to so lovingly pleasure me with her warm gentle mouth, she had also wordlessly reached over and released the clamp on the hose of the large bag she had brought to unwillingly fill me. The act had begun the slow but relentless and now inevitable release of all of its contents into me through the sealed stretched entrance just below her tenderly suckling lips and tongue.

Now I could see the flow meter slowly turning as I could feel my colon start to gently swell from the slowly growing pressure. Hearing the sound, the women at my breasts, as they continued to deliciously suckle my swollen and tingling nipples, reached down to start to massage my abdomen as well, gently kneading my internals from the outside, apparently to move the fluid around and help make room for it within me. Now I could feel pressure not just in my rectum, but moving higher up into my colon.

Though novel, I was surprised that the sensation wasn't unpleasant or torturous at all initially; in fact the now-increasing sense of fullness deep in my bowels, combined with the cunnilingus and breast sucking, was starting to transport me. Softly moaning in helpless pleasure, I closed my eyes, trying to get beyond caring about the humiliating situation or the audience. But he wouldn't let me.

"The creature is now feeling the lower intestines start to gradually fill and swell," I heard him announce.

"The bag isn't high above our ass hole; we are filling her guts slowly, because we want her to be able to hold it for a while. This isn't just pleasant warm water for a standard enema; we've put a couple cups of warm strong coffee in it. This will enhance all of her senses for her upcoming intense sexual activity, and fully waken her from the earlier sedative, if she wasn't already.

"As you may know, without the mediation and interference from stomach acids, drugs are rapidly absorbed into the bloodstream through the intestinal lining."

He was right again. As I felt my colon continue to expand from the growing pressure, everything was already starting to seem more focused and clear. But it also refocused me on my utter mortification at my powerless situation as I remained rigidly bound to the performance platform in front of an eager audience of dozens, as the warm liquid continued to flow into me through what I had always thought of as only an exit for such things.

"Yes," I reported, opening my eyes, seeing the flow meter continuing to slowly turn and the bag slowly shrink, as my bowels continued to helplessly shift and enlarge, while the women continued to gently massage and manipulate them.

"I'm feeling warm and full and...oh my god, my bald pussy feels so good in her mouth, and everything seems sharper."

"Very good, I hope she'll continue to enjoy it," he responded. "We want to keep the liquid in her long enough for the caffeine to take full effect. But at some point, she will start to cramp. This is not a punishment enema, in which the subject is filled and then forced to hold it, with severe penalties if they cannot.

"In this case, the immobilized creature's bowels are being slowly engorged; she can for the moment relax all of her internal muscles as well as her bound external ones. For now, she can fully enjoy the women's mouths on our pussy and tits with no physical effort whatsoever, because the liquid cannot escape the tight seal we have stuck into and firmly embedded in our unwilling stretched ass hole.

"Speaking of sealed ass holes, Esmeralda, watching the two of you, and particularly viewing yours as you pleasure her with your mouth, has made me quite hard."

He turned around from the audience to face us.

"Please remove your plug so that I may properly enjoy this end of you while she does the other."

Supporting herself with one hand in response, the woman reached back behind herself with the other one as she continued to gently mouth my genitals. She withdrew the plug from what seemed to be a well-oiled anal passage, stretching the sphincter momentarily as she pulled it through, and put it in the jar of lubricant. Then, open, it narrowed. He stepped forward and, grabbing and spreading her well-formed buttocks with his hands, quickly replaced it with his large firm penis, stretching it again.

As he started to pump his hardened swollen member in and out through her now-clutching anal passage, she then took both her hands and placed them on my inner thighs, spreading my swollen vulva and sensitive vagina even wider in her soft warm lips, now humming and vibrating my genitals with the pleasure of the strokes in her rear.

Still completely immobilized, feet behind head, I continued to feel my vulva and breasts being licked and sucked, and my intestines slowly fill and shift and swell under the women's gentle hands, as I now watched on the monitor the slow ass fucking of the beautiful but cold woman whose warm mouth was currently buried in the tender crevice between my wide-spread legs.

The audience was watching as well, and some of them were clearly continuing to pleasure themselves. Now slowly growing used to the device that had widened and was uncontrollably flowing liquid through my own powerless anal passage, I started to grow curious about what she was experiencing, with the hard, warm, thick male organ (based on my brief recent experience with it in my vagina) slowly pistoning in and out of her tightly stretched muscular anal ring as she hummed her own apparent pleasure into my sensitive and swollen vulva.

As I considered it, I realized that I would probably soon know. And I was both appalled and strangely fascinated to also realize that I was slowly not only starting to accommodate myself to the notion, but actually starting to become even more sexually aroused by it. The thought and its implications were somewhat of a welcome distraction from the continuing enlargement of my abdomen as the drugged liquid continued to slowly but relentlessly flow into me with no ability on my part to stop it.

Unfortunately, the distraction was brief. After a couple more minutes, as he continued to pump his thick penis in and out of her tight exit to her continuing hums of passion, I heard him remark, "Esmeralda, the creature's bag appears to be empty."

Still hanging in front of my eyes looking straight ahead, I could also see that it was shrunken, no longer bulging. The turning flow meter had become motionless, and the vessel's contents had apparently been completely transferred into me through the tightly sealed stretched muscular ring between my splayed legs, below her suckling and licking mouth. I couldn't look down directly, but a monitor showed that my abdomen itself was now uncomfortably distended, swollen as the bag had previously been, making me appear slightly pregnant. But at least I had apparently been able to accept it all without bursting which, at this point, I considered a small victory over these seemingly heartless people.

"Now close the clamp and disconnect her hose."

Without interrupting either her cunnilingus of me or her continued clutching of the hard penis continuing to slide in and out of her own stretched anus, she put a hand down to support herself once again, and reached down with the other to obey his command. I heard the click of the clamp closing, and then another one as I felt a little jerk in my own now-sensitive sphincter from the disconnection.

As he continued to stroke in and out of her, repeatedly burying and emptying and reburying his thick member deep in her rectum, he announced, "The creature is now full and completely sealed. We will continue to let the caffeine take effect."

9

=====
THE RELEASE

The hose now disconnected from the swollen nozzle still firmly embedded in and stretching my exposed anus, I was now completely sealed up with the unwanted coffee enema uncomfortably distending my bowels and expanding my belly. I remained fully immobilized, my thighs spread wide, feet still rigidly bound behind my head and my wrists frozen at my sides. This was occurring in front of a crowd of complete strangers, as the beautiful blonde woman continued to pleasurably lick and suck my genitals while a large firm penis was slowly and deeply sinking into and then sliding out of her own rear entrance. I could never have previously imagined being in such a bizarre and mortifying situation.

I was feeling ever more awake and alert from the caffeine being absorbed into my bloodstream from my swollen intestines, and softly moaning as I enjoyed the gentle female mouths on my vulva and breasts and even feeling, perversely to me under the kinky circumstances, a sexual climax growing ahead. But the intestinal discomfort was getting more and more urgent; I could sense that I was going to start to cramp soon from my full bowels.

I was also getting concerned and wondering when and how I would be released from my bondage to be allowed to go to the toilet and empty myself but, remembering my recent punishment, was terrified to ask.

"I love the licking and sucking, but I am starting to cramp," I decided to dutifully report, hoping almost desperately that it would prompt them to let me go.

"I also feel like I am going to come soon."

After I added the final few words, I immediately regretted it. Hearing them, the man reached forward even as he continued to slide his penis in and out through Esmeralda's own stretched tight sphincter, grabbed her hair and pulled her soft warm mouth back away from my blood-engorged tingling lower lips and clitoris. "Oh, no, we can't have that, not yet," he exclaimed. Then he released her.

"Esmeralda, let us play a little game with her. Put your tongue just a fraction of an inch from our swollen clit."

The delicious suction at the equally swollen nipples of my breasts had ceased as well as he had pulled her mouth away from my vulva. As she obeyed him, continuing in her silence and seemingly without regret or compassion, I cried out, "Oh god, please! Please let me have it!"

"As you can see," he remarked to the crowd, "Esmeralda's tongue is right there. It looks to be just in reach; perhaps the lusting creature will entertain us by straining herself forward for it."

Because the other women had also lifted their mouths from my breasts, I was now left with no erogenous stimulation whatsoever other than the continued stretching of my virgin anal sphincter by the ballooned enema nozzle.

Despite the still-growing intestinal distress, that I was utterly unable to relieve due to the tight lubricated nozzle stretching and sealing my exit, I pushed down on my bound wrists and strained against the waist strap, attempting to renew the stimulation between my legs.

I was desperate to shift my crotch forward to feel her warm soft tongue again, and relieve the deep sexual tension and now indescribable hunger in my groin, unlike anything I'd ever felt before in my life. But between the waist strap she had tightened on me, and my bound arms and feet holding my thighs back, and my own weight sticking my upper ass to the platform, I couldn't budge it at all.

"You see, a perfect example of how her immobilized situation tantalizes and frustrates her," he lectured, without interrupting the stroking of his thick member in and out of the woman's clenching stretched anal sphincter.

"Observe how she now desperately seeks the intense sexual pleasure awaiting her, like a wanton slut.

"Well, we won't torment and deprive her much longer. Nora, go and fetch the creature her receptacle, which I think she will find most welcome at this point."

With the words, he removed one of his hands that had been spreading the woman's buttocks as he had been slowly thrusting in and out of her. With it, he reached into the lube jar and retrieved the anal plug that she had removed from herself earlier. Then fully withdrawing from her own still-tightly clutching anus, he replaced his penis with it, apparently with neither of them having reached completion. The ring restretched as he shoved it through, then she squeezed it and pulled it back inside herself.

In my renewed terror and humiliation, as I was trying to comprehend the meaning of his last request to the assistant, he stepped back, and quickly pulled on a pair of rubber gloves as Nora approached them with a large, deep bucket. Apparently I hadn't misheard, and its appearance created a sudden sinking feeling in my swollen gut; I didn't want to even think about why she had brought it.

"All right, Esmeralda, step aside, and take over for Nora at the other tit. We'll take it from here."

The woman dismounted from the bench, moved the enema stand back out of the way, and came around to my right side to replace the other woman at my breast, though neither resumed suckling me.

"We are going to give the creature relief now, and perhaps the most intense orgasms she's ever experienced, whether she wants it or not, though right now she seems desperately eager and even begging for it. I am fairly confident that, in the process, the intensity will cause her to completely lose control of our tight new anal sphincter and thus her bowels, which is of course a necessary part of the process of cleansing them for our mutual future pleasure. In fact, when it happens, this would be good time for her to void her bladder as well if she has a need, while we have the bucket in place in front of our lovely multiple holes between her helplessly spread legs."

My body still frozen in my tight bondage, I listened to him in a state of complete shock and disbelief; this was rapidly becoming a nightmare. Earlier, as Esmeralda had attached the enema bag to the unremovable nozzle in my now-stretched anus that he had previously inserted and she had inflated in my rectum, I'd thought my situation couldn't possibly get worse, but it was clearly about to.

My previous humiliation was nothing compared to what was to soon occur as I realized, with his words and the presence of the bucket, that I was to remain rigidly bound in place in full view of everyone and the cameras as I both sexually climaxed and violently expelled all the fluids within me through my shorn naked anus and urethra below. It might even be recorded.

I was to not only have no privacy whatsoever to satisfy my urgent need to empty my unwillingly engorged intestines, and bladder, but it was apparently to be a key feature of the "performance" for which I was supposedly to be financially compensated. I had never anticipated anything like this when I'd signed up for this crazy gig.

Stunned, I thought again about the safe phrase, but as he continued to lecture to the audience about me in the third person, like a depraved zookeeper, I remembered the money, and finally decided to steel myself for the coming profound if irrational embarrassment from an utterly terrifying situation over which I had absolutely no control, short of sacrificing a significant amount of cash.

"Again, ladies and gentlemen," he continued, totally ignoring what had to be a clear expression of dismay and even despair on my face at his words, "you saw earlier that, by rigidly binding and thus immobilizing the limbs, we have ensured that no significant muscles will be in play for the creature except internal ones. If you watch carefully, you will see clear signs of the creature's powerful initial climax in the seemingly agonized, yet in fact intensely pleasured grimace of her beautiful face at both the sexual ecstasy and intestinal relief. Perhaps the fingers and toes will tightly curl as we unavoidably compel her to finally and intensely come repeatedly; we didn't bind them.

"But most of the interesting action will be in the deliciously spread crevice with our clenching orifices between the creature's lovely thighs. The profundity of the climaxes as we forcibly stimulate her will inevitably open their floodgates – the sluices of her juices, so to speak – and she will involuntarily and rapidly discharge her abundant and now unbearable internal fluids through them.

"While the high-velocity flow of liquid from our straining distended ass hole will be obvious as we force the first pent-up orgasm out of her, watch more carefully for the blossoming of our currently clenched cunt as she comes, with our pussy lips still swollen from desire and Esmeralda's mouth, and even now we can see squeezing and hungering in futility for something not presently within it."

Continuing to be completely immobilized and still utterly unable to prevent it, I watched and felt him reach down with two fingers and spread me just below my clitoris, providing a clear view of my urethral exit in closeup in a monitor.

"Also observe above our ravenous squeezing cunt the much smaller pee hole, which will probably be strongly streaming piss as the tightly bound creature violently and likely loudly comes and helplessly spasms in her rigid bindings for our entertainment.

"I will try to not interfere with the flow of the latter into the bucket as I stimulate her just above it. But I should caution that, while I've heard that some people are into that sort of thing, as at Sea World, people in the front are in the splash zone," he finished, with appreciative chuckles from the audience.

At the crude and graphic words of what was about to happen to me in front of a crowd of strangers, my stomach knotted even beyond that caused by the intestinal fullness, as he raised the kneeling bench out of the way so that he and Nora could get closer to me with the bucket. I groaned helplessly again in my renewed and even greater mortification, and painful frustration at the insistent twisting of my guts and the deeply aching need for completion between my rigidly bound spread thighs.

My feeling of total powerlessness was also reaching new heights with each inevitable and terrible part of the "preparation."

"Get ready, ladies," he announced, probably to them, not to me.

It was his only warning. Nora held up the bucket in front of my exposed orifices, now desperate to expel the fluids paining my insides, regardless of an audience, at an angle apparently meant to maximize capture of the liquid about to be forcibly ejected from me.

I heard a buzzing sound begin as I felt him deflate the enlarged inner plug, and I then experienced the brief pleasure of him finally slowly removing the now-slender device that had been so uncomfortably stretching my sphincter. It slid out of me through my now-sensitive anal passage as I continued to tightly clutch it in fear and intestinal pain, continuing to seal the fluid within me, just as Nora had earlier sealed the melting tranquilizer inside my rectum with her finger in the limousine.

Just as it was almost all the way out, the pleasure was suddenly either interrupted, or enhanced, depending on one's point of view, as he verbally signaled, "Now."

"Unnngggggggaaaaaaaaaaaaaaaaaaaaaa!"

I had never groaned so loudly or deeply or incoherently. I felt no longer human; I seemed, just as he had almost been describing, a wild animal, uncontrolled other than by my rigid bondage.

The long-awaited orgasm was like a massive electric shock convulsing my entire being, as a jet of brown liquid involuntarily rocketed out of my straining and stretching fundament straight into the bucket.

My immobilized body was racked with the extremity of the climax that had been pent up within me almost since I had first been bound, with all the psychological and physical stimulation since.

It had resulted from the tender still-swollen tips of my breasts being simultaneously re-enveloped in the women's soft warm mouths on his command as his hand had suddenly pressed what was apparently a powerful vibrator against my exposed defenseless clitoris, after the previous minutes of teasing and deprivation. The sudden unexpected exquisite sensation on my most-sensitive sexual organ, itself still engorged and firm with blood and tingling from Esmeralda's previous gentle sucking and tonguing, had been almost unbearably accentuated by the pressure of the fluid in my bowels and bladder.

The powerful stream had forced the rest of the nozzle out of my anus as its first act, as he took it away in his gloved hand. As he had predicted, I felt myself totally losing bladder control as well, screaming at the intense unprecedented, almost torturous vibration against my swollen clitoris, combining a strong pungent stream of urine with the fierce outflow from my distended sphincter. He withdrew the vibrator momentarily as I gasped repeatedly from the sudden exertion, but my breasts continue to be gently sucked.

After a few seconds, as I continued to pant in exhaustion, he observed, "That was very good, but I think she has more to go," as he applied the wand to me once more.

"Oh my fucking god!" I screamed, as the next orgasm uncontrollably crashed over my body like a powerful ocean wave, and more hot liquid violently erupted from my ass into the bucket, mixed with more bladder output.

He kept powerfully humming my swollen clitoris as, eyes clenched shut, toes curled and fingers involuntarily balled into tight bound fists, I helplessly racked myself over and over, unable to move anything else except my diaphragm, anus, and bladder, and lips and tongue, almost unable to process what was happening to me.

But what surprised me, in some recess of my mind, was that in the tortured ecstasy of my sudden forced violent orgasms, and the accompanying humiliating rapid involuntary semi-public emptying of my lower internals through my usually private exits, the thought of my safe phrase had somehow never even entered it.

The breast suckling stopped temporarily as Nora took the fouled bucket away, and I briefly thought the ordeal was over. Then it resumed.

"We will wait a bit for the intestines to rearrange, and get the last of the liquid out of her," he announced, as Dora brought another empty bucket, and he gently massaged my almost-empty belly, and bare vulva, as I continued to moan with a strange emotional amalgam of humiliation, intestinal pain and intense pleasure in my genitals.

After a couple more minutes of this, as she held the fresh bucket up to my holes, he applied the vibrator to me one more time as the other women took my nipples back into their suckling lips, eliciting an ultimate jet of fluid that had apparently been migrating down to my bowels' exit from upstream, with nothing left after but drips from my stretched sphincter into the angled receptacle, accompanied by another deep mindless groan from me.

Then finally, gradually, he released the pressure on my tender seat of sexual pleasure and lifted the buzzing wand away from my overstimulated groin.

Now I was breathing deeply as, eyes shut, I enjoyed the sensation of one of the women gently washing my tingling anus and still-swollen genitals with a warm damp cloth.

As I slowly recovered from the extremity of the final climax, I gradually became aware that the audience had been applauding. I also suddenly realized that what they were applauding was, among other things, and as he had predicted, the most intense orgasms of my relatively young life. It was as though they had been deeply buried within me from birth, and long waiting to finally be released. I also felt as if they had somehow opened a gateway to new even more powerful and pleasurable ones to come.

After another couple minutes, as I finally caught my breath, I felt his fingers massaging my vagina and clitoris again, and the deflated, cleaned and relubricated training device, the outer section still inflated, slowly reentering my rectum. This time he pumped it slowly and deep in and out, rhythmically, gently fucking my anus with it as he again stretched and stroked my vagina with his fingers above it. But this time, rather than attempt to push it out or resist as I had before, I almost automatically started to squeeze with new-found anal muscles I'd never previously exercised, and moaned again with the new sensation.

"As you can see, despite the creature's earlier concern, she is starting to discover the intense joys of anal penetration and stimulation. There now is no resistance to my arm, and the device slides in and out of our tight ass hole readily, as she tightly clutches both it and my fingers in our warm delicious cunt in obvious pleasure.

"It is now time to expand her anal horizons."

Hearing the words, to my shock, I realized that I no longer necessarily disagreed.

10

THE RINSE AND REPEAT

Though I was glowing in the aftermath of the most powerful orgasms of my life, now fully awake from the caffeine that had been absorbed through my intestines, and relieved to be now empty of the fluid that had been forced into me below, I remained spread wide and rigidly bound, the intimate shorn holes between my legs still on full display to the crowd of strangers and the cameras. The device that had previously stretched my sphincter and enabled the undesired filling of my bowels continued to slide pleasurably through my anal passage, in and out, tingling nerves that I had never before realized were there. After all my previous fear, I was now shocked that the stroking and stretching of my anus could be so pleasurable.

But then it stopped, buried deep in me again after another full insertion.

Once again, as he pumped the bulb, I felt it start to reinflate inside my rectum, with a renewed sense of dismay. Though the gentle slender anal fucking had felt surprisingly good, even without the genital massage, I had thought the enema portion of the preparation was complete. As I felt below my retightened and tender anus being restretched and resealed, I knew it was not.

"We can see from the facial expression that the creature is less than thrilled at the prospect of being refilled, but at least this time she's smart enough to avoid complaint."

His remark came as another enema bag was wheeled in, this time by Dora. This one was yellow, and at least as large and bulging full as the previous one. As before, I felt the click transmitted through the nerves of my now-hyper-sensitive sphincter as she silently attached its hose to the nozzle once again swollen at both ends of my anal passage. Equally silently, still helplessly, I now girded myself.

"We will give her a little while to rest the interior muscles. Dora, it's your turn to pleasure her now."

As Esmeralda had earlier, the beautiful young woman lowered the kneeling bench, climbed aboard, spread me with her hands, and started to massage my still-swollen vulva with her own soft warm mouth. The camera showed that she too was still ass plugged, as she had been when introduced. Esmeralda and Nora were continuing to suckle at my breasts as well. This went on for a few minutes, as my diaphragm and other abdominal muscles continued to relax from their recent violent exertions.

But too shortly after I fell back into the mindless pleasure of the vulva licking and nipple sucking, eyes closed, trying to pretend there was no audience, softly moaning again, I heard the click of the clamp being opened. Once again I felt warm liquid start to slowly flow through my anal passage into my lower intestines, to inevitably refill them, and I could feel the pressure start to build up again in my bowels. This time, however, I at least felt I had a better sense of what lay ahead, and was feeling less concerned and frightened, and even a little less embarrassed, knowing that I had gotten through it once.

"Dora, please unplug, and show our guest how much you also enjoy the feel of a large hard cock sliding in and out of your own stretched ass hole."

Without hesitation and, as with Esmeralda, not interrupting her cunnilingus of me, the woman put a hand down to support herself, and reached back behind herself with the other to pull out the plug. But unlike Esmeralda, she didn't remove it at once. She made a show of it; I didn't know whether for the audience or for me.

Despite my bizarre humiliating situation, fully naked with feet still rigidly bound behind my head, I watched in fascination on the close up in the monitor as she tugged it out only partially, then pulled it back into herself with a reclench of her sphincter, then back out, back and forth, a little further each time, stretching her ring wider with each pull. And each greater enlargement created hums and moans of her own apparent pleasure with the motions and stretches of her anal ring, which in turn vibrated her mouth on my clitoris and bare-shaven genital lips, sending repeated paroxysms of more pleasure from them up my spine. So I guess it was at least partly for me.

She finally pulled it all the way out, revealing a larger plug than Esmeralda's, and a gaping wide relaxed anal cavity, into which the large firm penis was quickly inserted without resistance. He gave a gentle slap to her right buttock, apparently as a signal, as though he was giddy upping a horse, and the wide sphincter instantly clamped closed on his thick member. Feeling her grab it, he spread the buttocks with his hands and started to slowly pump his penis in and out of her as he had with Esmeralda. As with Esmeralda, I could feel her own new moans of pleasure on my lower lips with each stroke.

"Though you can see that she was quite wide upon removal of her toy, Dora exercises her anal ring regularly, and is now clutching my cock quite tightly, and clearly enjoying it as she continues to pleasure the subject with her mouth. Some of you who have paid the requisite ticket price may soon experience her anal talents yourselves.

"Our bound beauty, on the other hand, is experiencing a new sensation in addition to the stimulation of our tits and pussy. As the liquid slowly flows again through our restretched ass hole, she is likely feeling a slight burning in the gently swelling colon. We have given her a different cocktail for her tail this time. In addition to warm water to rinse, she is getting half a bottle of fortified white wine, along with a cup of olive oil – virgin, of course – to fully lubricate the bowels and make it easier for us to later pleasurably slide our cocks in and out of our eager stretched, tingling tightly clutching sphincter."

He went on, accompanied by laughter from the audience, "I will note the wine is not an expensive vintage, as its unlikely that our ass hole has that discerning a palate.

"We are again filling her gradually as she is building to another orgasm, and the alcohol in the wine is being rapidly absorbed into the bloodstream as it enters the bowels. Each beat of the strong young heart carries it quickly to the brain, and she is probably already feeling a little tipsy. The drug will have at least two effects: It will relax all the muscles of the bound body, to help prepare our still-tight anal ring for the needed further stretching for our coming entertainment. It will also reduce the inhibitions that have prevented her from fully accepting the preparation, resulting in her own greater enjoyment of the intense sensual and sexual activities inevitably to come."

As he spoke the still-crude but now-arousing words, I could indeed feel the slight sting in my intestines, and the effects of the alcohol.

The coffee had heightened my senses too much for it to dull them, but I was relaxing more and simply accepting the feeling of growing intestinal fullness combined with the continued ministrations of Dora's mouth on my again-throbbing genitals. It was accentuated by the continued tugging at my breasts from the other women's soft tongues and lips as they again massaged my abdomen to help move the fluid into my intestines. The memory of the recent applause from the audience, despite the bizarre involuntary feats of my body that had prompted it, almost made me feel like an actual star of a performance.

"As the alcohol takes effect on the creature, and the useful interior muscles relax even as the exterior ones remain useless to her, we will now inflate the neck a little more, further widening its diameter."

As he spoke, the woman reached down just below her mouth to gently pump both bulbs a few times.

"It can get a good bit larger, and it will continue to further expand our deliciously tight ass hole, as part of the ongoing process of converting it into a proper receptacle for our mutual lust and pleasure."

I moaned again as I felt the increased pressure on the muscles of my anal ring. There was a slight new stinging in my sphincter as it stretched again beyond its new current size, but it didn't last long, and the continual nipple sucking, and licking and sucking of the clitoris and my outer vaginal lips below them by Dora's humming mouth, as the large penis slid in and out of her own now-tight anal passage, were a transcendental distraction from it.

The liquid continued to gently but relentlessly reflow into me, and my bowels and belly continued to reswell with the drugged contents of the new bag.

As they did so, I continued to helplessly slip slowly into a more relaxed and slightly drunken state, feeling occasional slight increases in the diameter of my sphincter.

After a couple more minutes, I was gradually feeling another orgasm starting to build in my engorging bowels, and groin, and despite the continued graphic verbal reminders of my unwilling buggering soon to come, the thought of my safe phrase was at this point far from my mind. Eagerly looking forward to the coming sexual climax, I decided to not warn them this time, in order to maintain some semblance of control. With the next words I heard, though, I realized that it was, as when I was attempting to verbally avoid the first enema, to no avail.

The women assisting him had all been silent up to this point, but just as I was about to come again, the young woman raised her head from my snatch, in which her sweet warm mouth had been buried, and looked to him for guidance as his penis continued to stroke through her own clutching stretched anus.

"I think she's about to come again," she observed, in a soft but matter-of-fact voice – the first time I had ever heard it. "And her bag's empty."

"Back off, then. As before, we don't want to waste her orgasm when she can't fully relieve herself, and if we empty her out now, there won't have been sufficient time for the alcohol to have provided its full effect. We will want to continue to build the tension toward her next intense come, to properly empty and clean her again. Disconnect the hose and seal her up."

Once again, I groaned in frustration, still completely bound and unable to pleasure myself, but desperate for continued genital contact as she obediently removed her mouth from me. I heard and felt the now-familiar clicks of the hose clamp closing and hose being disconnected from the thick nozzle embedded in and stretching my tingling widened anal sphincter.

"The creature is full now, and sealed once again. See if the three of you can just keep her on edge, with light touches of tongue to clit and nips, while she continues to absorb the alcohol. I'm sure she would love to rub our swollen tingling pussy that Dora has been licking, but you have rendered her hands otherwise occupied."

There was another chuckle from the audience at the words.

Obediently, as she continued to pleasure the swollen male member still sliding in and out of her apparently well-trained anus, the young woman danced around my tender button with her tongue, as her beautiful ass-plugged colleagues continued to do the same at my breasts.

"Oh, god, please don't tease me. I can't take it," I groaned. "I have to empty, and I have to come."

The women ignored me, obeying him, and continued to provide just enough stimulation to keep me on the precipice of the climax, but not allow me to go over. My sense of drunkenness slowly continued to increase from the alcohol that continued to be absorbed into my blood-stream through my full lower intestines, though nowhere near to the point of insensibility. Along with the intoxica-tion, the urgency in my genitals continued to grow as well, almost beyond endurance.

Finally, when I thought I could take no more of either the sexual frustration or cramping, I heard the blessed words, "Nora, bring the next bucket."

"Oh, god, please hurry," I cried out, ignoring the warnings about complaints or requests in my new desperation for completion in my groin, and relief of my renewed intestinal distress.

Fortunately, this request was accepted without punishment. As he had spoken the words, he had withdrawn his penis from Dora's stretched clutching anus.

After quickly grabbing and reinserting the large plug in her empty bottom, she dismounted and restowed the bench, moving into position at the breast that Nora had abandoned to get the receptacle.

Several seconds later, Nora arrived and once again angled the vessel up to my exposed holes. As before, I felt the collapse of the seal of my bowels' exit, and then the sudden shock of the powerful vibrations on the most tender part of my swollen genitals as my breasts were taken fully again into the women's mouths on his command.

As I came again, and my intestines rapidly re-emptied, I screamed in a combination of relief and sexual ecstasy. This time, in my mild inebriation, the violence of the release of liquid made me feel like my guts themselves were being violently expelled into the bucket, and my whole body powerfully spasmed in its taut bindings as it never had before.

Once again, as after the first release, I panted, unable to see straight, almost recovering with a brief respite, when the vibrator was pressed home again, and more liquid jets erupted from both my distended anus, and urethra.

"Oh fuck oh god oh fuck oh god oh fuck oh god...!"

I continued my completely uncontrollable simultaneously obscene and profane unladylike cursing, indifferent, as with all else, to my audience at this point, almost incoherent in my unbearable pleasure as the ultimate fluid was expelled from my body by the previously unimaginable comprehensive stimulation of all in me that could be stimulated. It was a seeming total annihilation of my senses.

But finally, slowly, the intensity of the vibrations was first reduced, then the exquisite pressure on my swollen tortured clitoris was removed completely. The warm suction on my breasts and stimulation of my swollen nipples was ended. I started to regain comprehension from the extremity of my latest exhausting orgasms and compelled exertions and helpless evacuations of my internals.

11

THE WIDENING

Still completely immobilized, eyes closed, I continued to pant from the exertions of the most recent violently forced evacuation of my bowels simultaneously combined with the most intense orgasms of my life. But the frequency and depths of my breaths ultimately reduced, as the alcohol once again took precedence.

I opened my eyes as I heard the audience starting to applaud again as well but, this time, with a "shushing" gesture from the masked impresario, they stopped and just watched in impressed silence at what they'd just witnessed, as I started to breath more normally. I watched and felt a warm wet cloth once again gently cleaning my swollen vulva, and my anus, still burning from the so-rapid ejection of the drugged and oily liquid from my bowels.

I reclosed my eyes to try to ignore my continuing helpless and surreal situation, and practiced controlled deep breathing. I was interrupted only by a mouth again on my vulva, as I opened my eyes briefly to see that Nora had started to take her own turn, and then felt the other two women rotating on my breasts. In the limousine, she'd barely brushed my inner labia with her tongue, but now she enveloped all of my genitals in her soft warm lips. She gently licked first one tingling outer lip, then the other. I felt the apparently lengthy tongue then sink deep, in and out of my vagina. Then it massaged my swollen clitoris.

I could see in the monitors her own display of her shaved genitals and plugged anus to the rapt audience, the vulva opening and closing with apparent unsatisfied desire as she gently probed me with her tongue.

Each woman's oral technique was slightly different, and I again reclosed my eyes and gave myself over to the now-familiar pleasure. I was allowed to continue to bask in this manner as well as I could in my extreme bound and humiliated state, unalloyed by anal stimulation or intestine filling, for several minutes.

Then slowly, as I kept my eyes closed and, now slightly drunk, tried to pretend to myself that we were alone, and that I wasn't fully spread in front of a crowd of strangers and video cameras, I felt her fingers gently massaging my clitoris, as the tongue itself moved lower.

She first tenderly licked my perineum, up and down, from the upper border of the pucker of my anal sphincter to the bottom of my vaginal entrance. As she continued to rub my clitoris, such stimulation had never felt so good, even better than when she had caressed it with her fingers in the limo, sending new shivers up my spine. But after a minute or two of this bliss, she moved even lower, and started to even more delicately explore my recently violated anus with the tongue, slowly circling the ring of sensitive muscles, then softly probing at the center.

I could never have imagined the pleasure that was coming from what I would have previously considered such a disgusting act, but I groaned with new ecstasy at the stimulation of what now seemed like countless anal nerve endings, and continued to relax, allowing the strong and apparently long lingual muscle to enter my cleansed tunnel, gradually reopening and restretching me.

After a minute or so of this new intense pleasure, the woman lifted her head from me briefly.

"The combination of the wine and olive oil make for a nice ass-hole dressing, though I prefer vinaigrette," she remarked, in her gravelly sexy voice, to the laughter of the crowd, shocking me back into the surreal reality.

She then slipped her literally saucy tongue back into my relaxing anus and continued to gently thrust it in and out for a couple more minutes, as my groans of anal pleasure were now completely natural and unavoidable, and I gave myself over completely to the amazing new sensation.

"How has everyone enjoyed the performance so far?"

The thunderous applause of the audience this time thoroughly jolted me from my brief reverie.

He gestured to Nora, who promptly removed her tongue from the anus in which it was inserted, folded the bench back into the platform, and moved aside, out of his way, as the other women withdrew from my breasts. The tongue was then quickly replaced with three of his lubricated fingers which, as they had done earlier with my vagina, entered deep through my now-relaxing sphincter, spreading it once more, this time with no pain.

"As you can see, and I can feel, our new entrance of pleasure is now clean, lubed, relaxed and almost open for business," he declared. "It is time for her final training, and her not only willing, but eager granting of not only the previous visual, but future physical pleasure to us. But it will require further widening of our tight young sphincter.

"Nora, you haven't removed your own butt plug. Perhaps you might show it to our guest whom you've so eagerly been plumbing with your talented tongue."

Though she too had apparently been plugged the whole time, unlike the other women, she had never been given an opportunity to replace it with something more pleasing. She reached back and, without ceremony, removed it from her own anal orifice, and held it up to my eyes.

After Dora's extended performance in withdrawing her much larger one, it was much smaller than I had imagined. "*Even I could take that easily now*," I thought to myself.

"All right, Nora," he requested, "now share your little toy with your new friend, and push it into our new ass hole."

Ever obedient, the woman slowly slid the well-lubricated plug through my own immovable slick exposed anal passage, now not just growing used to, but almost welcoming such previously feared intrusions. The smaller toy slipped painlessly past the now well-oiled entrance into my rectum, to my unexpectedly great pleasure; I had felt empty since the removal of her tongue.

"Now attach the inflation bulb."

"*Oh, god, it's another expandable one*," I realized without saying it, wondering how big it would get.

I felt another little pleasant jerk in my now sublimely sensitive anus as the bulb was attached to the quick disconnect. Then I felt my rectum slowly refill and anal ring restretch and again widen as Nora gave it first one squeeze, then another.

As she did so, the man was putting a condom on his erect penis and lubricating it well.

"I am putting on protection because I am going to attend to our long-neglected cunt now, as we gradually increase the diameter of our anal ring beyond anything it has experienced before," he explained.

He placed the head of his hard thick shaft in its rubber sheath once again at the hairless entrance to my now-hungering vagina.

"I don't necessarily expect to come in her, but I don't want to take any chances, and even pre-cum can impregnate. We don't know her time of the month, and we don't want to leave her with any unexpected gifts of joy.

"Moreover, I don't want to have to worry about children of mine in the world that I don't know exist."

This last announcement came as he had already reentered me, and I involuntarily moaned with pleasure again as he started to slowly slide in and out as he had earlier, when I had been paralyzed with both my bindings and fright. Now, after each few delightful strokes of my stretched stuffed vagina, Nora reached underneath his testicles, which a camera angle showed were softly and rhythmically slapping against the flared end of the growing plug in my anus, as I could feel, and gave the bulb another slight squeeze. I was starting to feel full in my bottom again, but had become accustomed to the sensation from the earlier enema-nozzle inflations.

"I can feel the plug expanding nicely just inside the ass through the wall of our tight cunt," he announced, continuing to stroke. "I'm sure she's feeling our ass hole slowly but inevitably growing in diameter as well."

"Yes." I now took care with adjectives of ownership.

"It continues to sting a little each time the pressure increases and your ass hole gets widened for you, but then it seems to accommodate it. I'm getting a delicious feeling of fullness and pleasure in both of your tingling stretched holes, like nothing I've ever experienced."

It must have been the alcohol; I was shocking myself at the frank and almost clinical words coming so naturally out of my mouth in front of an audience of complete strangers while having another stranger's penis sliding in and out of my vagina with a swelling plug in my bottom.

Though I had to admit, in my slightly inebriated mind, with all that had occurred, he was rapidly becoming something other than a stranger.

"Very good."

His response came as he continued to slowly and deliciously thrust in and out of me.

"Nora, slowly continue to expand our tight ass hole to an inch and a half or so as I continue to stuff and stroke our eager clutching cunt. That will be a good average diameter that will allow it to accommodate larger things, once the creature has fully relaxed and accepted it. Ladies, please be once again attentive to our clit and tits, and we shall see if we can make her come again, more gently this time."

Nora rubbed my clitoris, and I felt once more the soft lips sucking at my nipples, increasing the already multiple sources of deliriously intense stimulation. I felt the diameter of my sphincter increase again with another squeeze of the bulb, as the penis continued to fill and empty and refill me, sending a continual indescribable tingling and shivers up and down my rigidly bound body, with an occasional complete withdrawal and tease at my vaginal entrance.

My ass felt as though it was being split by the growing intrusion in my taut anal ring from the expanding plug, but it was now a strangely good pain. He started to piston his penis into me harder and faster, as I grunted with each powerful thrust, and felt the climax building once again.

Nora continued to finger and massage my swollen clitoris above the rapidly stroking thick penis, now slamming hard against my pelvis. Then she gave one more squeeze of the bulb, enlarging my sphincter again almost beyond endurance. The final stretch resulted in a sudden explosion of incomprehensible ecstasy between my spread thighs, and in my full holes in my groin, causing me to close my eyes tight shut and curl my toes and fingers again.

With another incoherent groan, I squeezed the thrusting girthy male member in my vagina harder than ever before. I almost forced it out with the intensity, as the normally controlled man issued a deep animal howl of his own passion. I felt him jerk uncontrollably within me, and in some corner of my mind amid the chaos of my mindless pleasure I was glad that the semen would be contained. It hadn't been as violent or intense as my previous vibrator-forced orgasms, but it was much more satisfying.

He remained in me for a minute or so, as I continued to pant and recover from the latest orgasm, but more slowly with each breath, as I also became aware of the amount of stretching my sphincter was enduring. The plug was astonishingly big inside me now, but perhaps due to the alcohol, or the general post-climax relaxation, it didn't hurt.

I felt him shrink within me, then slowly withdraw. Then he removed and disposed of the latex barrier. My vagina once again felt barren, the feeling accentuated by the continuous sensation of the now-huge plug buried in my tingling clean and stuffed-full bottom.

Behind him, I could see that several audience members were continuing to self pleasure, and clearly some of them, including at least one woman, had climaxed themselves during the performance.

Slightly out of breath from his own orgasm, he proclaimed, "I believe that the subject's training is now almost complete. There will be a forty-five minute intermission to allow her to recover and refresh herself.

"Following that, she will physically demonstrate her new skills to those who pay the premium price. There will be further entertainment and an auction in the lobby while you wait."

With those words, the audience, some of whom had to first rebury their genitals in their pants, exited the theater, murmuring at what they had just seen and experienced, and in anticipation of the final act.

12

=====

THE INTERMISSION

As I continued to relax from my most recent intense orgasm, the theater was now empty other than the masked man, his three assistants, and the equipment to which I remained rigidly bound, naked and spread with a thick plug buried in my bottom and stretching my anus.

"All right, I'm sure she needs a break from her position. She is also probably dehydrated."

He was right; I had lost track of my now-obvious thirst and dry mouth in the extremities of the recent experiences.

"I am going out to continue to entertain the customers during the intermission, but I'm sure she'll be in good hands." With those brief words, he departed.

Nora brought me a plastic cup of some liquid, as Dora detached and lifted the band holding my head in place so that for the first time since the beginning of the show I had freedom of motion of it. Because my hands were still strapped to the platform, keeping them from my mouth, the woman held it up to my lips for me, and I started to drink it eagerly. It was sweet, but also had a strange and interesting bite to it. After a few swallows, I stopped. "Thank you. That's enough."

"No. Drink it all," she commanded. Her husky tone was now like ice. I looked at her face, which had taken on a cast of indifference.

After a pause, she continued, "That is not a request."

She nodded over to my left, indicating that she wanted me to view something. I turned my now-free head to do so, and saw on a stand the thin rod that had so astonishingly painfully struck my bound soles earlier.

"As you have already experienced, I can grant great pleasure, but we are all quite capable of inflicting cruel punishment if necessary, without causing permanent injury. My medical training helps. And unlike him, I actually enjoy doing so, and find it quite recreational."

After a shocked moment, I nodded in acknowledgment at the chilling words from the woman who had given me my pre-show examination and whose tongue had been stroking in and out of my now-stuffed rectum not very long before. But I was also surprised to hear the word, "you." It was the first time I had been addressed in the second person since his pre-show warning that I would not be.

I accepted the cup to my lips once again, this time continuing until it was empty.

"May I ask what you just gave me?"

"You may," she replied, still emotionless. "It is a combination of various berry juices. They contain anti-oxidants and some sugar to restore your energy, as well as electrolytes likely lost when you expelled so much fluid from your ass. It also contains a couple ounces of almost flavorless laboratory-grade ethanol. The initial glow of the wine enema is probably wearing off, and we are going to keep you slightly pleasantly drunk and relaxed, particularly to help you continue to accept the large object now widening your ass hole, and others, perhaps larger, to come."

On my otherwise empty stomach, the effect of the alcohol was indeed rapid. By the time the woman had finished speaking, I was already starting to feel a renewal of my inebriation, and my sphincter was continuing to relax and stretch wider with its new toy.

Finally, she smiled, breaking the tension of the previous dark mood. "He will not refer to you in the second person, but we may, out of ears of the audience."

"We are going to allow you to stretch. I'm sure you could use the relief, but don't try to take advantage of it, or you cannot imagine the punishment that would follow," she warned.

"Thank you."

My reply was quiet as I felt my feet being quickly unbound, and the release of the ratchets restraining my wrists, unwinding and loosening the tethers holding them enough for me to bring my forearms and hands together for the first time since I had awoken from the sedative.

With my arms now straight in front of me, one of the women slid out two horizontal rods that had apparently been embedded into the end of the platform. The cuffs holding my feet together were then unclipped from each other, my feet were released from behind my head for the first time since I'd awoken from the tranquilizer, and my legs were lowered to rest on the rods. They had rings along them, to one of which the ankle cuff on each leg was reclipped, presumably to keep me from escaping. But they then rotated the ends of the rods outward, spreading my legs along with them, and locked them into place. I realized now that their purpose was to keep me restrained while letting me stretch and rest my legs but still maintaining access for the women to what resided between them.

As before, Nora and Dora then held me up as the pole behind me was folded back down into the platform by Esmeralda, at which point I was gently lowered to lie flat on my back, my legs spread wide by the cuffs on the rods, and my still-tethered arms folded across my abdomen, the tethers now running loosely between and underneath my upper legs. The women pulled two more straps from the platform, each going over each of my shoulders and through my armpits, and cinched tightly to firmly hold my upper body down, while my waist remained strapped down from my initial binding.

"Here is a much better pillow than your feet."

Esmeralda gently held my head up and slipped it comfortably underneath. It was the first time I'd heard her crisp English voice since she had abducted me, and the first time she'd ever addressed me in such a kind tone.

It was the most comfortable I had been since I'd awoken from the sedative. I luxuriated in the ability to stretch my limbs. I had no idea how long I had been in that preposterous position, but it was a great relief to no longer be, even if only temporarily, and still largely restrained in my motions. My legs down, and now lying in a more traditional spread-eagle position, the flare of the plug was no longer exposed, but buried deep in the soft flesh of my ass cheeks, but I could still feel the girth of the neck in my now-widened anal sphincter. My shorn vulva continued to be exposed above it by my spread legs, and once again the women went to work on it and my breasts with their hands and mouths.

As I started to relax with my limbs finally stretched and the gentle womanly lips, tongues and fingers at my genitals and nipples, Esmeralda continued.

"As he said, the purpose of this intermission is to allow you to stretch something besides your arse hole, and prepare yourself to fulfill your training, and your agreement. We will keep the plug in you throughout, because we don't want your hole to shrink again after all the hard work that all of us, including you, have done to get it open. Note that we always wear ours during the performance except when something more fun is in our bums.

"We are going to keep you sexually aroused until it is time to put you back into the position for your coming vigorous buggering after the intermission. You may do whatever you wish during this period – nap, come, or just relax – but at the end of it, understand that the end result will be to have you immobilized again, and prepared to pleasure the pricks of the theater patrons with your trained, opened, cleaned and lubricated, tightly clutching arse hole, to satisfy them and your contract."

The gentle tone of the sexy voice was at odds with the surreal nature of the words, and the description was more than a little overwhelming.

"Will they all be fucking me in the...arse?"

I was trying to contemplate how long I would have to be bound in that condition.

"No, of course not. Quite a few are women, but even for just the men, that would take many hours, and despite whatever you might think about their moral depravity, these people have lives. This is a performance, not a lifestyle," she explained, with a smile.

"About a third of the men have paid well to bugger the three of us. Many have no opportunities for anal sex in their normal lives, and we're very good at it.

"We like it because there is no need for birth control. Also because...well...we intrinsically enjoy it and are very happy to get well paid for our own pleasure, particularly since, unlike you, we are able to rub our own quims as we tightly squeeze their pricks with our arse holes, though we didn't do that during your preparation because we had to focus on our jobs, and the main point was to excite both you and the audience for the upcoming anal activity.

"They'll be bringing in platforms for us right behind you, with stirrups like a gyno's table, so we can either kneel on them to be buggered from behind doggy style as he was doing to us while we licked between your legs, or lie on our backs with our feet in the stirrups and legs spread, whichever the patron desires. The platforms are adjustable in height, as this one is, to accommodate different heights of the patrons, or different bum-fucking positions for us.

"In your case, height would only be adjusted for the customer, since you'll remain firmly and helplessly bound in your upright leg-spread arse-bottom position as they enjoy stuffing their hard warm thick pricks into your stretched tight arse hole and stroking them in and out of you until they helplessly shoot their spunk deep into your bowels."

The words were disturbing but also, to my surprise and shame, after all I had gone through and with the continuing labial attention below, becoming arousing, as was probably her intent.

"You'll be able to watch us being deeply bum fucked as well on the monitors, if you need a distraction or another source of arousal in addition to the deep plunging of the thick prick in and out of your own stretched arse, though I'd advise that you concentrate on pleasing your own current customer, as I'll explain in a minute.

"You probably heard him say that there will be an auction during the intermission. You were well displayed to the bidders during your preparation and training, and their sexual appetites for you and particularly your arse were thoroughly whetted. The patrons of our establishment are generally wealthy, and the reason we can afford to pay you so much for a few hours work is that, as we speak, the pleasure of your tight sphincter is being offered to the top three highest bidders, and even then, we make a good profit. So with his initiation of your apparently virgin bum hole with his own prick, which from experience we can assure you that you'll enjoy, that will make four total intense arse fuckings for you after the intermission.

"The rest are just voyeurs, some of whom will wank off or, in the case of the women, simply rub one out as they watch us.

"The customers are limited in the length of their fucking either by the clock, or by their inability to prevent their come, whichever happens first. And we do whatever we can to make them come quickly, with both our anal muscles and verbal encouragement, so it won't go more than an hour or two maximum. You'd be advised to help yours as well if you want to minimize the time, and maximize the amount, that their thick pricks spend in your arse."

She spoke the last with another smile, and I laughed despite myself at the concluding double entendre. Despite the utter surreality of my circumstances, and despite the crude and graphic description of the events soon to occur, hearing her calm and soothing voice actually came as somewhat of a relief, at least in comparison to my original fear at the beginning, when I had first been bound, of being brutally ass fucked for hours or days.

And knowing that I'd have willing and even enthusiastic partners sharing my experience in the bizarre enterprise, I now felt that, as degrading and depraved as the situation would be, I might be able to handle it.

As I had been instructed, I closed my eyes and continued to breathe deeply and relax, and continued to let my lower orifice stretch for the upcoming anal festivities, in my mild intoxication from the alcohol and the less-mild one from the gentle licking and sucking of my most-sensitive erogenous zones.

After a few minutes of this blissful activity, as I could sense another orgasm gradually starting to build in my groin, I felt one of the women remove her mouth from my vulva. A few seconds later, I felt her gently but firmly take the top of my head and chin into her hands. Surprised, I opened my eyes to see Esmeralda looking down at me silently, her face almost perpendicular to mine, wearing an expression of yearning.

I'd always been a good judge of the pulchritude of women, since that was a key way I had to compete for men. But as a straight woman, it had always been as a theoretical visual aesthetic quality, like a beautiful landscape, not a sexual stimulus. Now, after all that had happened and, slightly drunk, so close up and framed in her long blonde hair I found her visage unimaginably lovely, even mesmerizing, and truly appreciated for the first time the effect such beauty might have on a man. That she was somewhat foreign also made her seem both more exotic and erotic.

She clearly felt the same about me. Her lustrous green eyes with the long dark lashes looked deeply into my own for several seconds, simultaneously lovingly and lustfully.

Then she slowly closed them and, continuing to hold my head in place, wordlessly lowered her soft lips to my face, surrounding my mouth with them. Her own mouth fully open, she started to softly lick my closed lips with her tongue, gently urging, seemingly beseeching them to part for it. As she was doing so, I could feel another woman leave my right breast and replace Esmeralda's lips and tongue between my legs with her own.

With my shoulders strapped down and her grip on my head, I couldn't avoid the contact on my mouth but, relaxed from the alcohol, I strangely felt no desire to. I had never kissed a woman on the mouth before, but there had been so many other things I'd never done before today that almost without thinking I simply responded to her own obvious desire, slowly spreading my own lips and fully accepting hers as I reclosed my own eyes.

Upon feeling the welcome, her tongue eagerly entered and sought out mine, as she pressed the soft warm flesh that had previously given me so much pleasure on my lips below now against my upper ones, open as wide as her own. No man had ever kissed me so passionately, as our ravenous tongues quickly found each other and, first delicately, then almost desperately, intermingled. Her mouth had an interesting flavor, which I realized must have been from between my own legs, from the lingering effects of when she had had my lower lips in it moments earlier.

As she continued to languorously kiss and tongue me with her soft mouth, still holding the top of my head, she released my chin and moved the freed hand back to massage the lonely breast that had just been abandoned, as my other one continued to be suckled by one of the other women.

I hummed in pleasure at the new sensation of the long deep kiss enhancing the other ongoing sensuous stimulations of my nipples, still-swollen vulva and stretched anal sphincter. Then I felt fingers gently stroking both of my ear lobes. I was now almost at a point at which I'd forgotten that I even had a safe phrase.

After a couple minutes of the overwhelming sensations throughout my body, now including my lips and tongue and ears, I could feel the next orgasm, at least my fourth in the last couple hours, not even counting the multiples in the intensity of the enema releases, approaching. It continued to build first slowly as it had begun to before the kiss, then explosively as I suddenly came hard again, in the mouths of both Esmeralda and whomever was servicing me at my other lips below, with another deep mindless groan.

After my last helpless bound leg-spread spasm of ecstasy, to my relief, the other women removed their mouths from my now-almost painfully sensitive nipples and genitals. But Esmeralda continued to lovingly and deeply kiss me and gently massage my breasts as I relaxed again in the glow of the alcohol and my latest climax.

After another couple minutes, she slowly released my lips from her own, lifted her mouth from mine, and asked, almost casually, "Would you like to taste us?"

13

=====

THE TASTING

It was a shocking question.

I had never even had my face, let alone my lips and tongue, close to another woman's genitals. But after all I had already gone through, including the recent deep kissing, my fascination at another new experience, along with all else in my body, was surprisingly aroused.

"We don't generally come from arse fucking alone, and that's pretty much all we get during the performance, other than what we do to ourselves, so the tension sort of builds up," Esmeralda explained. "We also get nothing resembling physical foreplay, because there isn't time."

She paused, perhaps wondering if I was understanding the implications of what she was saying.

"You are literally in a good position to please us with your own tongue and lips, if we squat on your face.

"If you'd like, we could even remove our plugs so you can taste our arse holes. We always clean thoroughly before the show," she continued, after a moment of my silence, implying that they had undergone their own pre-show enemas, though likely unforced and undrugged.

She paused again. "Also, if you're concerned, there's no spunk in either of our arses from when he buggered me and Dora. He didn't come in us because he had to preserve his hardness in order to fuck your cunt."

With the last words, it was nice to have ownership of my own genitals again, if only briefly. There was another long period of silence, as they returned to slow gentle love making with me, in no obvious hurry for a response.

The other women, perhaps a little jealous of Esmeralda after her kissing of me, now each took their own turns on my mouth, each more passionately and deeply and arousingly than the other, as though they were in a competition to please me. They didn't have to hold my head as Esmeralda first had; a little tipsy, my former inhibitions continuing to crumble, I willingly accepted each offered embrace of their lips and tried my best to reciprocate. I was surprised that it required no acting on my part, even after the earlier harsh words from Nora, whose capacity for and apparent love of providing pleasure clearly at least rivaled whatever was her ability and desire to inflict pain.

As they continued to make love to me, I finally replied, in a brief break in the intoxicating osculation as my genitals and breasts continued to be pleasured.

"I've never done anything like that."

I was coming to realize that they weren't making me an offer, but rather making of me a request; they had been seducing me, and were asking me to make love to them with my mouth, as they had been doing to and for me, during the performance and more recently.

Dora spoke up.

"I like being ass fucked, but there's nothing I love more than mouthing a woman's holes while my own are being licked and sucked," she enthused.

"As you briefly experienced at the beginning of the performance, the scent can be terribly arousing.

"We won't force you, though we could, because it isn't very satisfying if not done voluntarily. But it might help better arouse and prepare you for the coming activity, which is after all the purpose of this relaxing interlude."

I thought about it a little more.

"Why don't you just please each other? You're obviously very good at this."

"We're at work," Nora explained. "Our job is to service you right now, and we'd be falling down at it if we neglected that for our own personal pleasure. But what we're asking would fall within the job description, if it helped excite you. It's also fun to be with someone new, and you're very beautiful and sexy."

I thought some more, but realized that time was limited for the decision and, finally, overcome by curiosity, and perhaps to some degree the alcohol, announced, "All right, I'd like to try it."

Without another word, Esmeralda, who seemed to be the leader, climbed on the platform, facing toward the empty theater seats, feet on either side of my breasts. She had apparently been eagerly hoping I would assent.

She slowly squatted down over me with hands in front of her at the sides of my waist, and started to lower herself to my face, her flared shaved vulva open and just inches above my waiting mouth. I could see the swollen clitoris above the vagina; she had probably been rubbing it.

"Start with the clit," she commanded. "I assume you know where it is."

After a pause, she realized, "Oh, bugger, I know you can't move much; just stick out your tongue, and I'll do the work and help pleasure myself on it."

Obediently, given my constrained situation, I stuck my tongue out from below as far as I could, and the woman shifted around until she felt it, then positioned her engorged sexual organ directly over it.

"All right, move the tongue up and down against it."

As I started to do so, I was staring right at the plugged anus, through which his penis had been stroking and stretching it not long before, an inch from my eyes. The flare of the plug covered her perineum, and the open vagina in between was just above my nose. It was hard to believe that I was looking so closely between the legs of the conservatively dressed cold woman who had accosted me on the street earlier, then pleasured and ultimately abducted me. The view and the aroma as I started to lick her genitals were in fact surprisingly arousing to me.

"Yes, that's it," the words came from above, with a moan of pleasure. There was little flavor to the hardened fleshy nub, but there was a great deal of scent from the love hole in which my nose was now almost buried.

After a minute or so, the woman shifted her lower body forward slightly so that my tongue could explore her labia and vagina. "Oh, yeah," she groaned, as my tongue entered her, and she lowered herself to get it deeper.

Now I could taste the vaginal juices. The flavor had a not-unpleasant tang, but she had probably cleaned that orifice before the show as well. I wondered if my own tasted similar. I pulled my tongue back momentarily so I could speak.

"I like the taste, I think. Do all women taste like this?"

She laughed at the question; the sound was almost musical.

"I couldn't tell you; I've only tasted an infinitesimal percentage of them. There are some things in common, and some things unique to each one. But there are two other women here, so you have at least a small sample to attempt to answer the question by induction."

She continued after a minute or so as I continued to lick her vulva and vagina, "Speaking of which, this feels wonderful, but the other girls need their turn, and I don't think I'll have time to come. Would you like to taste my arse hole now?"

I hesitated.

This seemed like some kind of point of no return on the road to utter perdition and perversion. It had been a strangely long journey for a young straight woman whose last normal memory just a few hours previously was leaving a yoga session.

But thinking about what had already happened to me in the past couple hours, and what was to come, and how much pleasure these women had given to not just my genitals, but my breasts and my own anus with their own tongues, I felt almost weirdly obligated to do it.

I finally replied.

"All right. Yes, I'd like to taste your ass hole," shocking myself again at the words coming from my own mouth.

The woman reached behind herself, raised her bottom slightly away from my waiting face, and slowly removed the plug just above my eyes, stretching it momentarily wider like before, as she pulled it through the muscular ring. Now, in its absence, the cavity didn't appear to be the normal tight wrinkled sphincter entrance, but open and round, and a healthy pink at the edges and dark inside.

"As you can see, the plug has kept me spread. I'm currently relaxed to keep it that way, which is a technique you'll learn as well. It's fun to open a tight arse hole with a tongue, but I'm sure I'm gaping wide right now. Would you like me to tighten up and close it so you can re-open it, or just lick the inside?"

Boldly and, admittedly, slightly drunkenly, I decided, "I want to put my tongue in it, and for you to tighten on it." Having completing the words, I stuck the organ straight up again toward the open orifice.

Without a word or hesitation, the woman lowered herself onto the waiting lingual probe, and let it enter her. From below, I gingerly circled it slowly inside the rim of the anal ring. There was a musky smell, but not a terrible taste. The owner of the orifice issued a hum of pleasure from above. After a few more seconds, she asked, "Are you ready for me to grab it?"

"Uhhnng huh," came my grunt from below, unable to say anything more intelligible with my primary muscle of speech sticking out and up in another woman's ass. In response, I felt the muscular ring quickly contract around it, trapping it inside. I tried to stick my tongue in deeper, and the woman lowered herself further against my mouth to help. Now curious, I enclosed my lips around the tightened sphincter, and sucked hard on the surrounding flesh.

"Oh, fuck, that feels great," she exclaimed. "I know you can't talk right now, but see if you can stroke it in and out. But don't take it all the way out."

Still providing suction to the whole area around her sensitive squeezing anal ring, I thrust the tongue as deeply as I could into the now-tight passage, then pulled it almost out, and repeated it.

The tongue that had been so deliciously engaged in sensuous combat with the one in this beautiful woman's mouth just a few minutes before, was now plunging gently but deeply in and out of her exit.

Dora was right; the thought of what I was doing to the creature whose aromatic genitals were directly above my chin was strangely arousing me. It was no doubt enhanced by the continuous licking between my thighs by one of the other women, and breast massaging and suckling by the other, combined with the sensation of the large swollen plug buried in the flesh of my buttocks and my own rectum, and stretched anal ring. Not to mention the alcohol.

As my tongue slowly stroked in and out of her anus, Esmeralda was rubbing her own clitoris, faster and harder and faster, until she suddenly clenched all the muscles between her legs with a seemingly uncontrollable groan of pleasure, helplessly forcing the lingual muscle out of the suddenly closed sphincter as though she were excreting it.

After a few seconds of panting from the apparently unexpected orgasm, she sighed, "God, I didn't know I had that in me right now. Pretty good for a beginner."

"Now, for practice, put the plug back in me, to reopen and keep me open for the performance."

Because my arms were still bound, she reached down from above and put the flare end of the still-greasy plug into my mouth. Once I understood what was happening I held it straight up in my teeth, supported by my tongue behind it, as the now-tightened anus was slowly lowered onto it. Though the plug blocked my view of the whole ring, I could watch the top of the sphincter gradually reopen as the woman above continued to slowly impale herself on it, with another groan of satisfaction.

Once past the point of greatest diameter, it suddenly popped back into her rectum as she sensed and clenched it, pulling it out of my teeth. From below, I gently licked the flesh surrounding the flare of the plug for a bit. Neck tired, I then laid my head back down on the pillow.

"OK ladies, it's your turn," she announced, dismounting both my face and the platform. "I think you'll enjoy it."

Nora climbed aboard next, except she decided to stand above my head and waiting face below, so as she spread her cheeks and lowered her crotch to my mouth, my view was from top to bottom, clitoris to plugged sphincter. Like Esmeralda, she lowered her sensitive sexual organ to my firm upright tongue, which then eagerly massaged it up and down and side to side, then in circular motions, though I couldn't see or smell the vagina or anus now below my chin, giving me no new insight into the variety of taste or smell of other women's private parts.

The woman issued hums of quiet pleasure at the lingual attention on her lower lips but, after a minute or so, told me, "We really don't have a lot of time."

She reached down like Esmeralda, raised up slightly, and slowly pulled out the plug, which looked larger than the one with which she had gifted me that was currently buried deep in my own rectum, stretching my anus wide.

"Now I'm going to tighten my butt, then move forward. You'll be able to briefly sample my dripping cunt with your tongue, and nose, but I really want to feel you open my closed ass hole wide with it."

Following through, she shifted her crotch forward to put her vagina over my still-busy mouth, which moved to the new fragrant target.

"Esmeralda was right. You do have a similar taste and smell, but it's different as well," I remarked as I briefly removed my tongue and lips from her pleasantly pungent vulva. "Almost sort of a floral scent, perhaps with hints of berries. It's an interesting flavor."

"Thanks for the *Wine Spectator* review of my cunt juice, but that's just the pre-show douche. Or the cocktail I gave you...OK, now here's my ass hole. You can see I closed it, so see if you can get your tongue in. I won't fight you," came the words from above as she shifted forward a bit more to put it directly above my tongue.

My nose was now in Nora's vagina and fully taking in her womanly aroma, as my tongue started to lick the tightened sphincter.

I started by circling it, as I had felt the woman above me do to me earlier (to my surprised pleasure), then slowly spiraled in toward the tiny hole at the wrinkled center. I was rewarded with a sigh of pleasure from her in turn. I started to gently probe the entrance, and felt the ring relax to allow my stiffened tongue to enter it. I continued to spiral from within the center, increasing the upward pressure, as it continued to slowly open and allow me to get into it deeper and deeper, even as I continued to be deliriously distracted by the soft mouths on my labia and right breast and massaging hand on my left one. Though with the woman squatting above my face totally blocking my view, I had no idea who was doing what to me.

Nora had started to massage her own clitoris, and was starting to pump her ass slowly up and down as she felt my tongue enter and open her from below. "Fuck, yeah, you're doing that like you were born to it," she groaned, moaning pleasurably as she rocked on my face.

She sat down more firmly on my eager mouth, which prompted it to start to seal up the area and suck at it as I had with Esmeralda, while continuing to stroke my tongue in and out of her loosening and opening entrance.

"Jesus," she cried, "yeah, suck my tingling ass, and fuck my tight ass hole with your tongue."

As before, I was continuing to be serviced at my own vulva and breasts by the other women, as I continued to satisfy the one above me with my own mouth.

Nora's fingers on her own genitals were getting more frantic as my tongue continued to slide in and out of her anus, and her vagina started to clench on my nose, which was buried in it.

Suddenly, my whole upper face was deluged in a very wet orgasm from above as she almost smothered and drowned me with her uncontrolled moans, pulsating flesh and fragrant flowing juices. I started to panic and gag, because I couldn't move my shoulders or use my still-bound hands to raise the climaxing woman from my face, my tongue still buried in her clenching anus. But Esmeralda, seeing what was happening while apparently still servicing my breasts, quickly jumped into action, pulling her colleague off of me even as the spasms continued.

"OK," she laughed, apparently amused at the mess, "So do you want us to clean you up now, or do you want to wait until Dora has drenched your face, too?"

I didn't respond immediately, still trying to both physically and emotionally absorb what had just happened.

"No point in cleaning me up if it's just going to happen again," I finally replied, trying to calm down from the brief fright, and starting to laugh at the situation myself.

"I don't tend to squirt like that, but now it's my turn," Dora demanded, who was removing her own large plug as she climbed aboard.

"We don't have a lot of time," she commanded, as she squatted and lowered her vagina to my mouth. "Don't bother with my clit, just taste my cunt for comparison and your dubious scientific research, then tongue my ass hole like you did theirs. You must have some kind of magic in that crazy-assed thing."

I sucked and licked at her dripping vagina, tasting the juices, and swirling them with my tongue. "You seem a little more sour," I remarked, "but I like it too."

"Different women have slightly different body chemistry, and it also varies with time of the month, time of the day, state of health, both genitally and generally, and level of arousal," she clinically lectured from above. "OK, now open my ass hole with that tongue like you did Nora's."

She was sliding forward as she spoke, positioning her now-clenched anus over my mouth. Feeling expert now, I spiraled my tongue in on the center as before, and once again started to pressure the tight ring, and was again rewarded with a relaxation and gradual opening of it, accompanied by her audible groan of desire. She had already started to rub the clitoris just above my eyes with her fingers.

I continued to probe, circle and stretch the relaxing sphincter with my tongue, as it got wider. Like the other women had, she settled lower onto my mouth, and I started dutifully applying the suction as I stroked in and out. "Oh, fuck," she sighed, and continued to massage her genitals above my eyes. I could smell her vagina strongly now, with my nose in it.

Now she was starting to clench the wet entrance around my nose, and each time she did, I felt the pressure on my tongue in her anus as well, but I continued to force it in and out, as I also continued to feel the other women's lips and tongues on my own erogenous zones.

She knew there wasn't a lot of time, but she also knew how to please herself, and within another couple of minutes, she was moaning and tightening all between her legs, forcing my tongue out of her sphincter as Esmeralda had. It didn't drench me as Nora had, but she did get my nose more wet as she groaned out her orgasm on my face. She raised herself off of me so I could breathe, and slowly moved forward and sat down on the platform above my head, urging a few last spasms out of herself with her fingers. After a couple of minutes, her own breath back to normal, she dismounted with a parting sigh of pleasure.

As she had been finishing, the other women had quickly set about gently cleaning up the aromatic mess on my face, and the platform. Then, they went back to licking and sucking my breasts and genitals, getting and then keeping me in a high state of arousal. But before I had time to come again, the theater lights started to flash on and off.

"That's the four-minute warning before the doors reopen, and cameras are running again," Esmeralda explained. "Time to get you ready for the rest of the show."

The moment I'd been both dreading and, in some warped part of my mind, curiously anticipating, was about to arrive. Before I could even think to object, my shoulder straps were quickly released and I was lifted up as before. Once again, I heard the post raised behind me and locked firmly into place.

I rested against it as they unclipped my ankles from the rods below. Then they helped me raise each of my legs once again so that my feet were again behind my head, then reclipped together.

As Esmeralda rotated the rods straight out as before, and slid them back in, out of the way for the performance, I felt my feet being recrossed and tightly rebound together and to the post by Dora and Nora.

As they continued behind me, I heard the clicking of the ratchets on the tethers on my wrists being recinched by Esmeralda, pressing my forearms once again against the back of my upper thighs. This contributed once again, along with my bound feet, to my renewed inability to lower them to protect my once-again spread, completely exposed shaven holes between my legs.

I was brought another cup of what I assumed was more spiked berry juice, and swallowed it all down as it was held to my lips, knowing better now than to question it, or anything. The head band was then put back in place and reattached to the post, and I could see only forward, as before. Also as before, this had all happened in the span of a couple minutes.

I suddenly realized the pressure in my bladder from the earlier juice, and perhaps absorbed fluid from the enemas.

"Do I have time to pee before we start?"

Wordlessly, Nora quickly went and brought another clean bucket, and angled it up to the exits in my overhanging crevice, as she had with the enema releases, then nodded for me to go. I relaxed, and let the urine flow freely with pleasure, as she gently massaged my swollen clitoris above my flowing urethra with her fingers.

I'd apparently abandoned all sense of embarrassment and shame at my bodily functions, at least with these women with whom I'd shockingly quickly become so intimately and emotionally, as well as literally bound. As I blissfully emptied my bladder, I could watch myself in the monitors, one of which showed my whole upright rigid body. The last drips of the urine expelled, Nora put down the bucket and, after quickly and gloriously licking me clean, took it away to wherever the others had gone.

As she had been helping me, the women at my sides had been completing the picture as before, splitting my hair under the rigid head band, draping it over each of my shoulders, and again liberating my breasts from under my tightly bound arms, to redisplay the aureoles, nipples in their center still swollen and hard from their own recent mouthing of them.

I looked almost like I had after the initial removal of the panties, except for one thing; my anus was no longer clenched, shut tight with fear. The other monitor was zoomed in on my crotch, and it now displayed my spread bald vulva with its blood-engorged lips, the vagina now looking hungry to be stuffed full again, and the swollen plug emerging from the exit that was now also an entrance below it. In some ways, it was an even more amazingly erotic sight. I had given up on imagining what a great job the video director and/or editor had, whether man or woman.

The women stood back to admire their handiwork.

"All right, you look great, and just in time," Nora declared, as the doors opened and the murmuring crowd noise could be heard once again.

14

THE INITIATION

The theater patrons started to flow back in and take their seats, again taking in the view that, to their eyes, hadn't changed since the intermission.

"I'd forgotten how hot she looked," one woman admired, almost enviously.

"I can't wait to replace that plug in the ass with my cock," one of the men enthused.

I could hear what was apparently the sound of the other platforms for Dora, Nora and Esmeralda being wheeled in and locked down behind my own, as I watched in the monitor.

Once everyone was seated, the masked impresario reentered the room.

"Well, ladies and gentleman, we are about to start the climax of the show, so to speak." The audience chuckled at the double entendre.

"Before we start, though, we have an interesting surprise for our young subject. As you know, the highest bidder turned out to be a woman."

He motioned to the right side of the audience, and an attractive older blonde at the end stood up and approached me and him. I recognized her as one of the women in the front row who had been pleasuring herself as she was watching the ass fucking and my earlier intense orgasms.

"I understand you didn't come prepared, but we can outfit you."

She nodded.

"Dora will fix you up; she has a lot of experience in fitting devices."

Dora asked the woman, "Would you like external only, or internal as well?"

"Internal," she replied.

"Both holes, or cunt only?"

"Both holes, please."

"All right," Dora responded, lowering the kneeling platform. "You'll have to remove your pants and any underwear, and climb up here, so I can examine, size, and prepare you."

The woman removed her shoes, then peeled down her own tight yoga pants and stepped out of them. She then slowly rolled down a thong as well, and climbed onto and kneeled on the platform, clearly aware from one of the monitors, whose camera was zooming in on her naked derriere, that she was giving the audience a show of her own. Her face was right in front of my immobilized snatch.

Dora dipped her hand in the jar of lubricant, then spread the woman's cheeks and the close up in a monitor showed her starting to massage the shaven genitals and anus.

"We have to do a little foreplay in order to prepare you to wear the devices," Dora explained as she kneaded and probed the woman's holes. She nodded in understanding, and then gave a sigh of pleasure.

"May I lick the pussy while you prepare me?"

Dora looked back at him with eyebrows raised.

He shrugged.

"Why not? You have paid a premium price."

There was lust in her eyes, and I gasped in sudden pleasure as she took all my bare vulva in her mouth and started to lick and suck at it, clearly no novice. She hummed against it as I watched Dora continue to massage and lubricate the woman's own vulva and anal passage from behind with the fingers of both hands.

"Do you know what size you like in your ass?"

The woman interrupted the cunnilingus briefly to reply, "Two inches is good. Same for my cunt." She paused. "And I'd like to fuck her with two inches." She then returned to mouthing my genitals.

Dora looked up at him again for guidance.

He responded, "All right, but you won't be able to go first; we'll have to work her up to that. But it should be no problem since you have already elected to go last and finish her off."

As the woman continued to pleasure me with her lips and tongue, Dora took a measurement of her waist with a tape, then continued to open and lubricate the orifices with her fingers to ready them for the coming much-larger intrusions. "Nora, go get three two inchers, with a number two harness."

Nora disappeared, returning a couple minutes later with three dildos with flared bottoms, and a thong-like garment with a hole in the crotch. She started to assemble it, inserting one of the dildos into the hole.

"You'll have to wear this until it's your turn; will that be a problem?"

Dora's inquiry came as she continued to lubricate and massage between the woman's rear cheeks. She lifted her head from my genitals again. "No, I will enjoy it. It will give me ample time to prepare me to pleasure us both."

"All right, the devices are ready, if you are."

She nodded as she continued to delightfully lick and suck at my swollen tingling vulva, circling and massaging my hardened clitoris with her practiced tongue. I and the audience watched in the monitors as Dora slowly pressed one of the dildos between the outer lips of the woman's vagina, with the camera zoomed in. Then she slowly pushed it all the way in as she continued to finger and widen the tight anus. As it entered, I could feel a hum again of pleasure through her upper lips on my lower ones. After a minute or so, Dora removed her fingers and gently pressed the other one against the entrance to the rectum.

"Are you sure you're ready for this?"

The woman lifted her head from me, and nodded again.

"Just go slowly. Give me a couple minutes to get it all into my ass."

Dora nodded in response, and slowly increased the pressure against the tight entrance. The camera was still zoomed in, and I watched in fascination as the woman seemed to push out against it, and the sphincter slowly bloomed to accept the rubber dong.

She stopped licking me again to ask, "Please, just hold it there for a minute."

Dora stopped, keeping it in place. After a dozen seconds or so, she requested, "OK, deeper now."

Dora pushed it in a little further. "All right," the woman announced after licking me for another half a minute, "the head is definitely past my anal ring. I think I can take it all the way now."

The rest of it was then fully eased into her stretched exit, up to the flare, as she issued a deep groan of mixed pain and pleasure into my genital lips. With both dildos now buried in the holes between the woman's legs, Dora then took the outfitted harness from Nora and declared, "All right, time to put it on. Let's see how it looks and fits."

With a sigh, the woman reluctantly abandoned my captive groin, and got off the platform. Standing up, she stepped into the harness with each foot, and Dora lifted it up, sealing the dildos inside her with the crotch strap, and tightening the belt around her waist. The third dildo was now emerging forward from her own crotch like an erect penis. My eyes widened at the sight, wondering how it would ever fit in my bottom. It was half an inch wider than the training plug in me now, which felt impossibly large.

"These are all vibrators," Dora explained. "Let's test them."

She pulled aside the tight thong-like strap between the woman's cheeks, and rotated the base on each one. The woman cried out, "Oh, fuck," and grabbed at the platform as her legs almost melted beneath her at the sudden sensations in her most private parts.

After a few seconds, Dora turned them off.

"All right, you seem to be good to go," Dora declared. "Please take your seat until it's your turn."

"Here is a towel to put on it, so you don't leak on the fabric while you're waiting," she continued as she handed it to her, to the apparent amusement of the audience. They openly laughed at her final warning: "And don't run down the batteries between now and then."

The woman smiled, took the towel, and returned to her seat, though her gait seemed a little awkward, which was unsurprising under the circumstances.

"All right, the time for the deflowering of our new ass hole has finally arrived," he announced, unzipping his pants and removing once more his hardening penis from them. "As her trainer, I will be doing the honors. I will start by removing the training plug, and replacing it with a holding plug, to keep our ass hole open for me."

He pressed a valve on my plug, and I felt it deflate. I moaned as it finally slid out of me, with a feeling of sudden emptiness. After having had it in there for well over an hour, I had almost accepted it as a part of my body, but it was quickly replaced with another firm large rubber one. I winced for a moment as it stretched me until it was inside, but then it seemed acceptable.

"As each of you enjoy her, you will first remove the plug from the ass hole, stick it in the lube jar, and immediately replace it with your cock, or for the lady, your dildo. When you have finished, you will equally immediately reinsert the lubricated plug *into* our ass hole, to keep it stretched and prepared for the next guest. The same will apply to those of you who have paid to enjoy the circular muscular talents of my lovely assistants.

"Before we start pleasuring our cleansed ass with our members, we want to make sure she is fully stimulated throughout." With the words, he brandished a short vibrator of ample girth.

It appeared to be more than two inches in diameter, larger than the ones the woman had accepted. It had straps on the end of it, and an electrical cord.

"We will keep our cunt stretched full and wide as we fuck our tight ass hole, to keep all of the only muscles available to her fully engaged," he continued, as he slowly stuffed it into my fully exposed and spread vagina, completely burying it in me as I moaned in pleasure.

It was wider than anything I had ever had there, but so sexually stimulated was I by the events of the past hours, I seemed to stretch easily and it pleasingly filled me without pain. He took the straps, threaded them under my backward-pointing legs, like my waist strap, and attached them to hooks on the platform next to my hips. Then he cinched them tight.

"These will hold the device in her, regardless of the strength of her orgasmic exertions, which I've experienced myself recently."

The last words were delivered with a smile.

"It is corded, because a battery-powered device wouldn't last throughout the performance."

He reached down and plugged it into an electrical outlet on the side of the platform.

"As a result, it is also quite powerful, but we won't run it at full power inside the subject; it would probably kill her from the excruciating pleasure.

"It will run at a lower setting to keep her in a continuous state of arousal as our tight clutching ass hole and our hard thick cocks mutually pleasure each other. Also since, unlike during the preparation, her assistants will be otherwise occupied, we will have to provide an alternate stimulus to the creature's nipples."

He held up a clear tube a couple inches in diameter with a handle on the end attached to a threaded internal plunger, and lubricated the rim of it. He placed it against my right breast, almost covering the aureole. As he held it down with one hand he turned the handle with the other; it slid the rubber-sealed plunger within away from my skin and apparently increased the effective volume. I gasped as I could feel my swollen nipple being sucked into it.

He released it from his hands, and it remained in place, apparently held there against gravity by the partial vacuum that was drawing the blood into my now rock-hard nub through the tender skin. He then did the same thing with the other breast.

Paralyzed by both the bindings and the overwhelming sensations in my vagina, anus and now breasts, I realized that the moment of truth must be arriving; for the first time in my life, I was about to have a thick warm hard penis stroke deeply in and out of my stretched and now-hungry anal sphincter.

"I don't know if the creature is ready or not, but it doesn't really matter because, as with all else, we, not her, are in total control, and about to begin."

My insides knotted from a mix of fear and excitement at the words, but I had no time to anticipate it, because I was suddenly jolted in my swollen genitals as he started the vibrator.

"Oh my fucking god!"

I wondered how powerful it could be if this was a low setting. I'd never felt such vibrations in my groin, and it was almost overwhelming, but the sensation was quickly augmented by what came next just below it.

As I was being stimulated just above, I felt my anus stretch further once again as he removed my holding plug, and then I felt the head of his hardened member, this time without the condom, pressed against my lower entrance, that until the past couple hours I had thought of only as an exit. My nipples were throbbing from the suction and my vibrating vagina was stuffed full and now on fire with desire as I awaited the sensation of being fucked in the ass.

Remembering what Esmeralda had said, I tried to relax my lower hole so he didn't have to reopen it, and was apparently successful, because he slid it in slowly, eliciting a deep groan of pleasure from both of us as the thick head of his penis slipped past my stretched anal ring.

After almost a minute of luxurious slow intrusion, he finally pushed it in all the way, his pelvis pressed against the sensitive skin surrounding my shorn widened anus. I had never felt so full between my legs.

"As you can see on the monitor, I am now buried in our ass balls deep."

Now that it was safely in, not having to worry about keeping myself open, I started to squeeze both the vibrator in my vagina and the warm meat stretching my sphincter, and was rewarded with another groan from him.

He kept it there for a minute or so, letting me adjust to the size and sensation, as I continued to squeeze it, then he slowly withdrew.

I groaned again at the new unexpected sensation. It was a strange good feeling, like relieving myself after a bad bout of constipation, except that after it was almost out, it came sliding back in again, refilling my rectum.

The nerves in my anal sphincter, now wider and tauter than it had ever been, were tingling unlike anything I had ever felt down there. I had never experienced sexual pleasure so intense, as he continued to stroke in and out of my now-eager and tightening anal passage. Occasionally, he would withdraw completely, and tease the entrance of my bowels with it, then just when I was at the point of begging for it and frustrated with having to relax to keep it open, he'd suddenly thrust it back in.

I couldn't actually climax, because it was as though I was in a continuous orgasmic state, and he was grunting with pleasure as well as he pumped his thick penis in and out of my formerly forbidden orifice over and over.

Eyes closed, I lost track of time, mindlessly, joyously clutching the sliding meat and vibrating rubber in my holes. But eventually I felt him jerk helplessly, repeatedly as he had earlier in my vagina, and I could almost sense the hot jets of semen erupting into my bowels, as he reached his release. As he came, I surprised myself with an amazing new plateau above any previous climax, and howled out my hardest orgasm yet, and of my life, my eyes rolling back into my immobilized head.

We were both gasping and panting, and I felt almost catatonic. Slowly, he reached up and turned off the vibrator, to my relief. He stood there, his member still buried in my rectum, but I could feel it slowly shrinking, and finally withdrawing. I felt a restretching as he replaced the plug, as I continued to slow my breath, and tried to relax.

Slightly out of breath himself, as before, to the applause of the audience, he announced, "Those who have paid for the privilege will find it well worth it. Despite her initial disobedience, the creature has been a spectacular student. This ass is now open for business."

15

=====

THE FIRST PATRON

With the surprisingly pleasurable end of my anal virginity, going by his announcement, it was apparently time for me to start to do what I had heretofore, perhaps irrationally, been dreading. I was finally about to please the high bidders from the auction with my newly trained anal muscles, while the other women did the same with their more experienced ones for those patrons who had paid for them before the show. It was apparently to be a four-(anal)ring orgiastic circus, with me as the star performer.

"The rules are very simple," he explained. "Those of you who have paid to indulge in our other ladies have been issued numbers, like at a deli, and the selection here, as you can see, is spectacular. You may fuck ass holes only. Any entrance in a cunt will end your experience."

The monitors showed Esmeralda and Dora lying on their backs on their platforms, the hairless crevices between their legs hanging over the ends and feet back far in the stirrups, their vulva spread and their plugs in place.

Nora was on her knees, shoulders down and head sideways on her platform, with her rear sticking out over the end of it, flare emerging from the stretched anus. Partially spread by one of her hands with all between her buttocks completely exposed, she was wiggling the beautiful bare plugged derriere back and forth invitingly.

All three women were massaging their own genitals with one of their hands and moaning softly with pleasure.

"You will be handed a half-hour timer which will start when your number comes up," he continued. "You may take your turn with whomever is available, and you may take her in whichever position you please. We will adjust the platform for your height and the position. If the woman you want is not available when your number comes up, you will have to let the next number go ahead while you wait for her current customer to finish.

"If you wish to change ass holes when one new to you becomes available, you may, but when your half hour is up, or when you've shot your load into one of them and shrunk, you're done. We will get the process going now, to excite both the audience and the star of our show before she begins her own performance."

I watched in the monitors, in a bizarre fascination, as a bell rang, and a board displayed first the number one, then two, then three. The apparent holders of those numbers walked up to the women's platforms, and were handed their timers by a new burly hooded man with a red beard, apparently another assistant. One of the first three took his place at Dora's platform, but the other two both seemed to want Esmeralda, so the one with the higher number stepped back and was replaced by number four, who seemed eager to fuck Nora's still-wiggling ass. The board switched to the number four. The timers of the three men were started.

As they continued to massage their own genitals, the women started to encourage the men, two of whom, at Dora's and Nora's platforms, had removed the plugs and started to stuff the tight anuses with their hard members.

I could hear words of "Open my ass hole with that big cock," "Slide it in and out, and stretch it wide," "Slam that meat in..."

Esmeralda's customer apparently wanted to take her doggy style as the impresario had, so there was a slight delay as she pulled her feet out of her stirrups, turned over onto her knees, and her platform was lowered to accommodate him. He then removed the plug and quickly replaced it in her bottom with his thick penis, with a deep groan of satisfaction. She squeezed it hard and cried out "Fuck, fuck, fuck, fuck my arse hole," as he eagerly stroked in and out of her stretched clutching sphincter.

The orgiastic sight and sounds of the penises plunging in and out of the anuses was apparently turning on the audience, many of whom had resumed self pleasuring. It was making me squeeze my vibrator and plug as well, and eager to start to finish off my own customers and finally end this and earn my money. After a few minutes of watching and listening to the busy buggering behind me, my first one approached me.

He was tall, of medium build, with dark hair, and not bad looking, as far as I could tell under the mask, and he came up to me with a pleased smile of eager anticipation. In other circumstances, at least based on appearances, I'd have considered dating him.

I could see that his penis was already hard, but not as thick as either the one that had just initiated my ass a few minutes before, or as my plug. His own timer was an electronic board on the wall next to the one displaying the anal-deli numbers for the other women, and as he reached me, it started to count down from thirty minutes by the second.

I gasped, and emitted another "Oh, fuck" as the thick vibrator strapped firmly into my vagina turned on with the beginning of the timer count, apparently automatically.

"After watching all you've been through, I'm going to really enjoy sliding my hard dick in and out of your tight ass hole," he smiled, as he gently tugged on my plug.

"You bet you are," I replied, with what I hoped was a sexy lascivious smile of my own. I'd been listening to and becoming inspired by the foul language and commands the women behind me were issuing as the penises stroked through their own anal passages.

"I don't have all night," I commanded. "Grease yourself up, pull that thing out of my ass hole, and get your big dick in it. Listening to all that ass fucking behind me, I need some hard moving hot meat, not motionless rubber."

I gave a grunt as he momentarily stretched me with the gentle pull of the plug, and put it in the jar, then took some of the lube from it and slathered it onto his hardness. As I had the last time, I relaxed to keep my sphincter open, and felt him easily enter me. I didn't wait for him to slowly work it in this time; the lesser girth was such that I figured I could start squeezing as soon as the head of the penis had entered, and I was right.

"Oh, fuck," he exclaimed, feeling my pressure, then thrusting it deep. "Oh, fuck that's tight," he cried out as he then slowly pulled it out. As before, the once-strange sensation of something sliding in and out of my rectum, as I squeezed it tightly, tingling even more all the newly discovered nerves in my anus, was now feeling glorious. The combination of vibrations in my vagina and the stretching of my sphincter again felt better than I could have ever previously imagined.

"Of course it's tight," I replied, as I kept using my new-found anal muscles on it like a new toy.

"It's so big it barely fits. You're splitting my fucking tight ass in half; it's going to break my ass hole," I lied.

He kept sliding in and out, then pulled it out and teased my entrance with it, saying, "I liked how they kept you from coming when you were getting your enemas."

"Cut out the small talk, and shove that big dick back into me," I ordered him, keeping myself open, and he obliged. "Shove it in and pull it out; make me come with a huge cock in my stretched tight ass hole. Pump it in and out and shoot my ass full of come," I shouted.

He was moaning with pleasure as he obeyed me, clearly excited by my continued loud and lewd encouragement, and I was too as I continued to squeeze and feel it stroking in and out. It hadn't even been seven minutes, but I could sense that he wouldn't last much longer.

"Fuck. Fuck! FUCK!" My exclamations came one word per stroke.

"It's so fucking deep in my ass I can feel that thing coming up my throat. I can almost taste the head of your dick. Your load is going to shoot right up my nose, or out of my fucking mouth," I cried as I continued to bear down on the penis pumping in and out of my now-eagerly tightly clutching sphincter. I was now realizing the pleasure that Esmeralda and Dora had been experiencing, except they'd had more girth, during my enemas.

He kept moaning with pleasure, and I kept squeezing his hard member with the excited muscles of my anus and berating him, which he also seemed to enjoy as he stroked it in and out of my clutching sphincter.

"You're not pumping me fast enough – shove that thick dick in and shoot me full," I yelled, as I continued to listen to the moaning and ass fucking behind me, from both men and women, as well as the latter's continued encouragement like my own.

In response to my commands, he sped up, slapping his pelvis against the sensitive skin surrounding my entrance, and I could feel him utter his own deep groan as his orgasm approached. His spasms in my tingling anus, combined with the continuous vibrations in my vagina, and the continuing suction on my breasts from the nipple suckers put me over the edge again as well, as I felt the next shipment of semen being unloaded deep into my rectum.

With the delivery, his body stiffened and he groaned even more deeply, remaining buried in me. I continued to squeeze my anal muscles, but could feel the shrinking of his penis, and my hole getting smaller with it. After a minute or so, now limp and soft, he finally withdrew, and stepped back. The vibrating in my vagina stopped as well.

"I need my butt plug to keep me open if you can't fill my ass with your cock any more, and I can't put it in myself," I admonished him, in a disapproving tone.

He sighed, picked it up out of the jar, and slowly slid it back into my rectum, as I winced again from the sudden stretch, but said nothing. "That was great."

"It was my pleasure," I replied with a smile, and I realized that the smile was in fact genuine; it had been. As I continued to listen to my new friends behind me continuing to service their customers in their own anal orgy, I was starting to feel like I could actually do this thing; one down, two to go. But my new-found confidence had come too soon.

16

=====

THE BREAKDOWN

As I momentarily basked in self congratulation after my initial success in the anal servicing of a patron, the next customer gave off bad vibes even as he started to approach me.

He was shorter than the first, with light-colored hair, and a scowl on his face. The seeming cause of the latter was his flaccid member, which he continued to stroke in apparent futility as he approached me, and I felt my platform being lowered to accommodate his smaller stature. The timer had restarted, counting down from thirty minutes, as had the vibrator in my vagina, shocking me with the initial jolt, as before.

"OK, cunt," he crudely declared, still attempting to get an erection. "I'm going to show you how an ass hole gets fucked, just as soon as my dick is ready."

He continued to masturbate, still in vain, and getting more frustrated by the minute. He painfully jerked the plug out of me.

"OK, let's see that ass hole I'm going to stuff."

But apparently the sight of my gaping anus seemed to do him no good. "You don't seem like that big a fucking deal, bitch," he complained.

"I don't know why you're worth all the money I paid for you. You can't even get me hard."

Now I was starting to get concerned. I didn't want to spend half an hour listening to this jerk berate and insult me for his own inability to get it up. I'd never considered myself an expert at fellatio, but I'd never gotten any complaints, and had often managed to rouse reluctant penises with my lips and tongue so, despite his crude tone, I tried to help with the only other muscle that was available to me for sexual activity.

"Hey, baby, lower the bench, stand up on it so you can reach my mouth, and I'll give you a nice blow job. I want to feel you stretch and fuck my tight ass hole with your big thick dick," I offered, as I tried to continue to relax the muscles below to keep it open despite the distracting vibrations in my full vagina.

He scowled again, but replied, "OK, bitch, but this had better work."

He got up on it after unfolding it, then climbed up onto the platform itself, standing with his feet at my sides, grabbing the pole behind me, and roughly shoved his soft member into my open mouth. He didn't smell or taste great, but I took him in and sucked on it, swirling my tongue around the soft shaft as he thrust in and out, but after a couple minutes, it was clear that it was to no avail, and he was becoming ever more angry.

He jumped down and slammed the bench up angrily, shouting "Stupid cunt, doesn't even know how to suck a dick."

He pressed the still-soft penis against my unplugged anus and perineum. "You get some vibes, so I'm going to try that, too." After a minute or so, as we shared the vibrations through the skin of my crotch, I could feel a little expansion in his member.

"OK, despite the fact that you don't turn anyone on, this is helping a little. I just need stronger vibes before I can shove my dick into your ugly ass," he insulted me again, as he reached down and, with no other warning, suddenly turned the vibrator up to full power.

The instant increase of stimulation in my groin was no longer stimulating; as the showman had warned, it was beyond painful, the worst thing I had endured so far. I almost felt like my genitals were on fire. I couldn't take it, and I started to scream.

"Shut the fuck up, you stupid cunt!"

As he shouted at me, he continued to press his semi-flaccid penis against my vibrating lower privates. Then, as I continued to scream, he muttered, more quietly, "I'll give you something to fucking scream about," as he started to swing his right hand back and forth at my face, hitting me hard, open palm on my left cheek and the back of his hand on my right.

Trapped in the head frame, I couldn't move to soften the blows, and with the combination of the unbearable torment in my groin and the beating of my helpless face, something broke down in my mind. I continued to scream, but in desperation, the screaming of pain was rapidly becoming articulated into words. And the words, repeated over and over, were "Code red!"

From when he turned up my vibrator to when he started beating me had all occurred within the period of a few seconds, and almost as soon as I started to scream my safe phrase, even more quickly than it had begun, the beating ended and the vibrator went silent, along with the rest of the room.

The assault had ceased when my tormentor had been violently thrown to the floor by one of the customers in the front row who had apparently and thankfully decided this wasn't going to be part of the program. He had then quickly pulled the plug of the vibrator from the socket in the platform.

Despite my relief at the sudden end of the torture of both ends of my folded bound body, I continued to repeat my safe phrase, but I was no longer screaming it. In the depths of my new despair at the realization that all I had endured so far was completely for naught, I was now sobbing the words, as a flood of tears now ran from my eyes down my stinging and aching cheeks, and dripped down onto my naked breasts below.

As I continued to weep inconsolably at the loss of my money with the use of my safe phrase, the man got up from the floor, shouting.

"What the fuck?! I paid good money, I'm ready now, and I'm going to fuck her ass. You know how it is, sometimes a guy's just got to slap a bitch around a little to get hard."

"You are done here."

The quiet statement was that of the showman, who had shown up from helping the other women immediately after the episode ended. He was accompanied by his new intimidating bearded assistant.

"We do not in fact know how that is. I supposed it is possible that there are establishments in which a vile sadistic man can pay money to brutally torture and beat a defenseless woman for sexual gratification, but if such exist, this is not one of them.

"See him out," he ordered his assistant.

"Goddamn you, you stole my money," the man shouted angrily, struggling in the arms of the burly bearded man on the way out the door.

"Refund him half his money, and retain the rest as a fine for damaging show property. And put him on the black-list."

I was shocked to realize that the English-accented voice that firmly spoke these last words was that of Esmeralda, who had suddenly appeared at my left side, with Nora at my right. Apparently the commotion had interrupted the carnival of anal carnality behind me. As she issued the order, she was gently wiping the tears from my bleary eyes with a warm damp cloth, and cleaning up my face.

"I'm going to report you," he shouted back at her.

"To whom?" she replied, sharply and loud, as she continued to gently clean me, despite my continued tears.

"The Better Business Bureau? The police?"

"I'm sure the latter will be quite fascinated to learn about your vicious assault, battery and torture of a help-lessly bound woman. We have dozens of witnesses. Perhaps you even have prior offenses?"

With the same scowl with which he had first approached me, he finally zipped his pants up, turned, and left the the-ater. As this was happening, Nora had started to gently probe my right cheek where he had cruelly backhanded me, as I winced through the tears.

"Nora really is a registered nurse," explained Esmeralda, who it was now clear was the one actually in charge of all; he was the showman, but she ran the business. "She has been responsible for all of your medications so far."

Continuing her careful, tender examination of my face, Nora finally spoke up.

"I don't have an X-ray here, but I'm pretty sure nothing is broken. But she's going to swell on the right side, and probably have a nasty bruise for a few days that she'll have to explain to friends and family. Dora, bring an ice pack, and 10 milligrams of hydrocodone and 300 of acetaminophen."

She then turned back to me.

"It's basically a generic vicodin for pain relief. The alcohol has worn off enough that it will be safe to mix. We're going to see if we can help you finish your performance."

As she was speaking, she had been re-lubricating the training plug that had been removed from me after the intermission. She once again eased it through my still-defenseless anus back into my rectum, and started to gently reinflate it. Being empty, my sphincter had clenched tightly closed from all the previous fright and pain, and apparently needed reopening if I was to continue to accommodate anything in it.

Hearing the words, and feeling the renewing intrusion below, I started to weep again at the thought of having to continue without being paid, and knowing I was still completely bound and powerless to prevent it. My tears continued to flow as they removed the frame so I could finally move my head, and Dora gave me pills with some water, then started to gently press and hold the ice pack against my now-swelling right cheek. Nora continued to pump the bulb and I could feel the plug slowly stretching my anal entrance again. As she pumped, with the fingers of her other hand, she tenderly massaged the swollen clitoris above the thick vibrator still embedded deep in my vagina.

"I know it hurts at both ends," she explained quietly, "but the painkiller and ice will help in a few minutes, and the show can go on."

After a long pause, as I continued to weep quietly in utter despair, Esmeralda spoke.

"I don't think that's why she's crying."

Her voice was gentle, but firm.

"I want you to listen to me."

As I ignored her, still sobbing inconsolably, she took my chin and upper head in her hands as she had during the intermission before she'd kissed me. She turned my now-freed aching face toward her own, as Dora moved her hand with it to keep the ice pack in place. Her voice became sharper and more insistent.

"Listen to me!"

Shocked by the tone, I stopped sobbing for a moment and, blinking, looked at her, once again into her beautiful green eyes.

"This wasn't your fault."

The words, in her crisp English accent, were once again tender. I continued to look at her through still-welling tears.

"It wasn't your fault. It was ours. We try to vet all the patrons, but sometimes someone slips through. That happened here, and we let it get out of control. And in our carelessness, though you'll heal quickly, it violated the spirit of the agreement to not injure you.

"I assure you, you didn't forfeit your pay with the use of your safe phrase. Of course we wouldn't expect you to take that kind of punishment without using it.

"Now blow."

She held a tissue up to my dripping nose. Thankful, I cleared it though, with the pain in my right cheek, I winced from doing so.

"If you can continue and satisfy the remaining customers, you'll get not just the money promised, but half of what we kept from him, as combat pay.

"We understand that, to whatever degree it existed, the erotic mood has been broken for you, at least temporarily. But if the pain subsides sufficiently in a few minutes with the ice pack and painkiller, and your sphincter is comfortably reopened, will that be acceptable?"

As the import of what the woman, who had been so recently so loving to me, was telling me set in, I stared at her in disbelief for a few seconds, eyes and face still wet with tears. Then I quickly nodded my head up and down silently, in relief, and elation.

17

=====

THE RECOVERY

As I was slowly recovering from the brutal assault, and the pain medication was starting to take effect as Dora continued to hold the ice pack to my aching right cheek, the showman turned to the masked man who had saved me, and had continued to stand by with a look of concern.

"I believe you were the fourth-highest bidder. Am I correct?"

He nodded.

"Are you still interested, under the circumstances, and still willing to pay your bid?"

He thought about it for a few moments, then replied, "Yes, she's still unbearably compelling to me, but she's been through a lot. I'd hate to just take her in her current state. I'd like to let her rest, and recover somewhat. I'd also like to pleasure her with my own mouth as she recovers, before I take her, if she could be cleaned up a bit."

"I agree. I'd also like that, and for her to tell me what she'd like."

The voice came from the woman who had been the highest bidder, still sitting in the front row with her strap on and internal vibrators, and had wanted to take me last.

After a few moments, Esmeralda gently asked me, "Is that what you would like?"

"Would you perhaps like to please these last two patrons unbound? Do whatever they ask, in whatever position?"

"Please," I replied. "I want to satisfy my contract, and earn my money, but please let me think for a minute or so. I still hurt."

The words came as my eyes were still wet and my right cheek still throbbing, and not knowing what to do, or how to actually even think about it. Both of the patrons nodded, in apparent understanding.

"All right. But the show must go on, and we are going to go back to satisfying the other waiting patrons. When you've decided, tell these two what you'd like to do. They have paid for you, and we will be satisfied, in terms of your contract, with whatever you want, as long as it's mutually agreeable with them, and we will try to help with it."

While Dora now cleaned me up below with her tongue to comply with the patrons' request, continuing to pump the anal plug wider, Nora strapped the ice pack to my face with velcro around my head. She advised, "If it gets to be too much from the cold, anyone can take it off if you ask."

I nodded, and she and the other women went back to their previous anal occupations, as I could hear as I considered my situation. I knew that I shouldn't keep the patrons waiting, in keeping with my contract, and within a minute or two, decided.

"Yes, please, lick my pussy, as I try to re-open myself, and stop hurting. I'm sure I'll enjoy that, and I'd be happy to accept your cock in my ass in any position you'd like. I'm very grateful to you for your saving me from that true asshole."

He hesitated at the words, then he responded, though I remained completely bound other than my head, by gently holding and turning it with the ice pack attached to my still-aching right cheek by the velcro strap, and giving me a long, passionate kiss, that put to shame the previous ones from any of the women. It gave me a deep thrill, and fully renewed the former interest in my groin. He finally released my lips.

"I want very much to make love with you, and grant you great pleasure, within the rules of the club, particularly after all I've seen you go through tonight.

"But I have to ask. You seem like an intelligent young woman. Why did you do this? Why did you put yourself through this?"

As I processed the question, I found myself surprised at my own feelings about it. I had thought that Esmeralda's earlier question about whether I wanted to taste her and the other women the most shocking, but I suddenly realized that this was the really penetrating one. Despite my total vulnerability and powerless nakedness, with all of my most intimate bodily functions having been on full display in front of him and the other strangers, it was in fact the most personal and intimate one, because it was about me.

And in thinking about it, I completely broke down again in tears, despite the prospect of the useful money from this horrible gig, even more money than I had signed up for because of my unanticipated physical abuse, because I also suddenly felt that not just my current bound state and situation, but my life itself, was so hopeless and inescapable.

Finally, as I saw his astonishment at my physical response to his question, I verbally responded. "I'm not an intelligent woman at all. I'm a stupid one," I sobbed anew.

"I did this because I wasted so much time and money getting three quarters of a completely useless college degree, and am hopelessly in undischargeable debt, serving coffee at minimum wage to rich assholes like the one who just mercilessly beat me for his own gratification while I was completely defenseless.

"Because of my gullibility and stupidity in buying the government-subsidized bullshit about the intrinsic value of college, regardless of the degree, I've apparently become reduced to involuntarily violently evacuating my bowels in front of a crowd of strangers to attempt to even start to pay it off."

I was crying openly now, almost wailing, the tears pouring down my face once again.

He seemed alarmed, but also deeply concerned at my renewed and now-continuing weeping at what he may have at first thought was his seemingly innocuous question. He gently wiped the tears from my eyes.

After a minute or two of attempting to comfort me, and continuing to clean my face, as he continued to seem to think about it, he finally turned to the woman, who had been anxiously awaiting her opportunity to take me last, with her own holes stuffed with the large toys.

"She has somehow grown to be of much more value to me. If I pay you your bid, will you take her now, and let me have her after you"?

The woman pursed her lips, and thought for a few moments. She finally responded.

"I understand. Yes, I will take her now, and there is no need to reimburse me; I don't need the money. I was actually getting tired of waiting," she said with a smile.

"But I also want to start with my mouth on her pussy, as I briefly did earlier and, as I understand that she's not ready yet for her next ass fucking, I think that will work out well."

They both looked at me, and I didn't know what to do, but finally I nodded, my face still wet with the tears.

She approached me, and then she too gently wiped my face.

"Is this still an acceptable position for you? Because I still find it a huge turn on to see you so completely spread and open and helpless to me. It makes me envious of you, in fact. I'm now curious to know what it would be like to be in that situation myself. But I'll do what you want."

I thought about it a bit, the pain in my cheek finally starting to fade from the medication. Then, after half a minute or so, and no longer crying, I responded quietly.

"Actually, it's pretty much effortless for me, if you find it satisfactory. I've never had as intense orgasms in my life as I have had in this position for the past few hours, with no fatigue."

I was realizing, though, that part of the ache in my cheek was now from the cold itself.

"But I would appreciate it if you would remove my ice pack. I think that it's served its purpose."

She unstrapped it, setting it aside, then tenderly, as had the other women, started rubbing my tingling clitoris.

"May I also remove the vibe from your cunt?"

In thinking about it, under the circumstances, I found the question amusing. Between humming from the genital massage, I asked, with a smile, "How could I stop you?"

"I used the word 'may.' I was asking permission from you, not querying you about my physical ability to do so, or yours to prevent me," she responded with a smile of her own as she continued to massage my swollen organ below.

"Well, it's been several hours since I've been asked permission for anything and, as you saw, my one and only attempt at denial of it was severely punished. So you can understand that under the circumstances I considered it a strange request."

I smiled again as the pain continued to dissipate from my right cheek with the increasing effectiveness of the pain killer and now her removal of the ice pack.

Seeming to be pleased herself, she smiled in turn and unstrapped the device from its bindings beside my hips, slowly withdrew it from my vagina, and set it aside as well. I moaned again with the sensation of it sliding out, but suddenly felt empty there. But then, without asking, she lowered the kneeling platform, and remounted it, as she had earlier, and started to gently mouth my vulva once again, taking it all into her own soft warm mouth, stroking her tongue in and out of my vagina and over my clitoris.

I could see the devices buried deep in her own holes in the monitors, held in by her tight thong-like harness, as she gently licked and sucked and hummed with pleasure between my legs. If anything, it felt even better than it had earlier. The pain medication was also apparently making it easier for me to accept the renewed stretching of my anal sphincter, because I was barely noticing the expanded plug there. My breasts continued to be stimulated by the suction devices he had placed on my nipples earlier, and had never been removed. I was once again being transported by all the sensations assaulting my entire helpless body.

She looked up at me, and declared, gently, "I want to feel and taste you coming in my mouth, before we do anything else, if you can. I'm going to continue to stretch your ass wider with the training plug as I lick and suck you. I'll have to really open you up wide to accept my thick cock."

Looking up at the clock, I realized that it wasn't running; apparently, under the circumstances, the proprietors had decided to let these two high bidders do as they wished with me, with my permission, on their own time. This was happening even as I could hear and see the renewed anal orgy behind me, with the plunging of penises once again in and out of the tight clutching anuses of the other women, to the chorus of their renewed verbal encouragement. And, as I could see in the monitors, the remaining voyeuristic audience continue to view all, including my own almost soap-opera drama of the last several minutes, as some continued to manually pleasure themselves.

"Yes," I replied, now feeling in fact like a soap character in a very explicit live show, as it had been in the old days of television, with the situation more surreal than ever. "I'd very much like that, too. Judging by the fact that the clock isn't running, I don't think there's any longer a big hurry, but your mouth feels very very good, and I think it's likely to happen not very long from now.

"Please continue to lick and suck my pussy and pump the bulb of the plug buried in my ass, to make me helplessly come again, this time hard in your mouth, and open me up fully for you. Then I want you to stuff your huge strap-on cock into my tight ass hole, stretching it wide while you rub my clit, until I come one more time, even harder, as you do too, from the vibrating toys buried in your own stretched cunt and ass."

I was once again shocked at my own crude and lewd words, but they seemed to have the desired effect. Her mouth increased its eagerness of suction at my clitoris and labia, as her hands spread me even wider, to the degree that was even possible with my spread-leg restraints. As she did so, she continued to occasionally reach down to pump the bulb of the training plug in my anus, and it seemed to be growing impossibly large, beyond anything I'd ever felt from it before, but with the pain killer and my previous experience, it continued to be not just bearable, but perversely pleasurable.

My anal sphincter had never been stretched so wide, but between her enthusiastic genital sucking and the pain killer, it didn't hurt, but rather increasingly encouraged my fifth, or sixth, or, I had lost count, whatever, recent sexual climax. As she had requested, after a few more minutes, and once again completely ignoring the existence of the audience, I easily, screamingly groaned out yet another hard orgasm into her mouth below, even as I felt her give one more pump to the plug. My once-virgin sphincter now seemed to be wider than it had ever been.

She continued to sweetly suck at my genital lips, and after a minute or so, pulled her mouth away from me.

"Are you finally ready for the wide vibrating cock sticking out the front of my harness to be shoved and stuffed into your tight stretched ass? Because I've been wanting to do that for, I think, now almost an hour."

"Yes!" I immediately responded, thinking that, relaxed after my most recent hard come, and with everything between my legs once again thoroughly tingling, I'd never be more ready. "Yes, pull out my plug and push that thick thing hard against my ass hole! Now!"

She wasted no time in responding to my command, raising her head from my snatch, turning on the vibrator sticking forward out of her own crotch, and slathering lubricant along its whole length. Then she rapidly deflated the training plug and slid it out of my stretched sphincter. She didn't climb down from the kneeling bench, but remained on it on her knees as she shifted herself forward to press the head of the thick vibrating dildo against my anal entrance. As I felt the pressure and vibration of it against my now-empty lower orifice, I requested, "OK, shove it in."

"I am, but you have to help. You should also push, like you're trying to shit it out. I know it sounds wrong, but that's the only way you'll open your inner ring to accept something this large."

I followed her advice, and pushed back with my internal muscles, straining my muscular anal ring against the large dong as I had during the intense enema releases, as she pushed and increased the pressure against it. Almost miraculously, I felt myself expanding even wider as it then slowly entered and stretched me once again beyond anything I'd ever felt before.

"This is how I took the two incher that is currently in my own ass earlier," she explained, as she stopped just within the entrance. "Accept the initial entrance of the head, and relax, and get used to it. I'll give you a couple minutes."

It hurt, but it wasn't unbearable, and I tried to relax and let my anus widen beyond anything it had previously endured, as she stopped and rubbed my clitoris for a bit. After half a minute or two, she asked, "Is it getting better?"

"Yes," I replied, realizing that it was, slowly. "Give me a little more time."

After another minute or so, I felt like I was continuing to slowly accommodate it.

"OK, shove it in a little deeper."

I felt it continuing to enter me in response to my command. The pain had increased again with the deeper intrusion, so I reported, "OK, please stop, and let me relax and open a little more."

The motion stopped again, despite my powerlessness to prevent her from stuffing it in completely had she wished to. She seemed to understand my sensations, and continued to gently massage my clitoris as she had halted the entrance of the huge vibrating dong into my anal passage. I continued to feel it relax and accept the wide intrusion, and was amazed to start to almost feel the beginning of the approach of another orgasm, this one centered completely in my anus. The muscular ring was now stretched far beyond anything I had previously imagined I could have endured when this whole ordeal had begun hours earlier. After another minute or so, I announced, "All right, I think its time to give me my deep wide ass fucking that you paid so much for."

Without removing the dildo from my ass, she reached over, picked up the vibrator she had removed from me earlier, and I moaned as she slowly and luxuriously stuffed it back into my now-ravenous vagina, which stretched again to accommodate it. She reattached its restraints to keep me from forcing it out in my approaching passion. Checking that it was turned off, she plugged it back in to the electric outlet. I issued a deep groan of pleasure as she then turned it on and slowly increased the speed, so that both vibrators were humming in my stretched holes. I'd never felt anything so continually and pleasurably intense.

She reached back behind herself, and turned on the vibrators stuffing her own holes, one by one, repeating her earlier "Oh, fuck," when Dora had turned them on, but this time able to maintain her control on her knees. There was a grimace of pleasure on her face as she finally thrust her crotch forward toward me, and pushed the thick humming toy into me all the way, as she apparently squeezed the other vibrating machines with her own circular internal muscles, moaning. I groaned as well at this deepest, widest intrusion yet into my fully-stuffed rectum, as I felt the continual vibrations in my taut anal ring and stretched vagina.

Now we both silently and motionlessly enjoyed the intense sensations in the wide-stuffed holes between our legs for half a minute or so.

Finally, I requested, "All right, now please fuck me," and she responded by pulling her groin away from mine. My "Oh, fuck!!!" as I felt the huge shaft sliding out of my full rectum was my loudest yet, and the feeling of emptying was delicious. Just as it was almost out, I gasped as she then thrust it back in again hard, burying it deeply and refilling me, as I continued to feel the vibrations in my vagina and clitoris, and the ongoing suction on my nipples. The drug-subdued pain in my face was being completely washed away by the most extreme ecstasy I had ever felt in the tingling holes between my wide-spread legs, still extending back behind my head.

She was moaning helplessly as well as, eyes closed, she started to continually stroke all the way in and almost all the way out of my helpless ass, stretched wider and stuffed fuller than it had ever been, over and over, as she continued to feel the multiple vibrations in her own groin. I could feel her trembling in unimaginable pleasure.

Once in a while, she'd pull it out all the way, and I tried to keep myself gaping open with the only muscles available to me under the circumstances. She'd tease with the thick vibrating dong at the narrowing entrance, then plunge it home again, restretching me and resuming the delicious stroking, tingling uncountable nerves in my taut widened anal passage as I continued to moan, also squeezing and clutching and pushing at the thick vibrating toy in my stuffed vagina, as it continued to be firmly held into me by the strong straps.

In the mindless bliss of the ongoing thorough vibrating penetration of both my holes, I lost track of time as she continued to pleasantly slide the thick humming dong back and forth through my stretched nerve-rich anal sphincter, but she finally grew more urgent, and started to pound me faster. I encouraged her, "Yes, ram that thing in and out of my stretched ass hole! Shove it all the way up my fucking throat, and don't stop until we both explode!"

At the words, she reached behind me and grabbed my bound feet, still immovably tied to the post behind me, for support as she leaned in close to my face with her own, her blue eyes beneath her mask now seeming to glow brightly with lust. Her mouth was wide open, as her pounding and thrusting in and out of my anus continued below, and she clearly wanted to take mine into it. I bent my freed head forward to press her lips to my own, and closed my eyes, as our tongues quickly found each other in a long deep kiss. I was getting even more excited at the thought of her mouth probing mine in the upper end of my alimentary tract, as I continued to feel myself being emptied and refilled at the other, as though she was indeed sliding through my entire ecstatic body.

I could feel her starting to spasm in her own groin as she was now clutching the wide humming toys in her holes uncontrollably, while continuing to thrust and kiss me harder than ever. As a result, I lost control as well, squeezing what was vibrating between my legs, including her dong sliding in and out of me, more tightly than ever before in my life.

When I had come in Esmeralda's mouth earlier, she had only been pleasing me, but now, so intimately connected with this woman at both ends of our bodies, we each groaned and grunted our climactic passion down each others throats. As she continued to explosively come seemingly non-stop, she set off my own next orgasm, then orgasms, that seemed now to emanate from and radiate out into my body almost completely from my stuffed squeezing exquisitely sensitive anus, then climbing up and exploding in my head like firework rockets rising from below.

I don't know how long we continued to climax, or how many times, as she continued to clutch me at both ends and kiss me and violently fuck my eager ass, but eventually, she slowed, and finally came to a stop, panting, with the dildo still buried deep in my rectum. I was breathing heavily, too.

After a couple minutes, as our breaths grew slower, I breathed softly, joking, "That was really great, but I didn't feel any fluid shoot into my ass when you came, like it did with the guys."

"There are current limits to technology," she smiled.

"But I actually like being a woman, and only do this sort of thing occasionally. Though this time it was amazing, worth every penny that I bid for you.

"I do, though, sometimes wonder what it would be like to be a man, and actually feel the sensation of a woman's orifice eagerly squeezing me as I ejaculate into her.

"But I had a great, memorable time. Thank you."

The last words came as she had slowly withdrawn from me, and I felt my still-gaping sphincter slowly shrinking, relaxing from its recent extreme exercise.

"Please replace my holding plug, to keep me open for him?"

She nodded, and silently responded to my request, removing it from the lube jar, and gently, almost wistfully inserting it back into my still-tingling anus.

"By the way, you don't have to thank me," I said, smiling. "You paid for it." Then, as I saw the look on her face with my last words, I immediately felt terrible.

"I'm sorry, I didn't mean that! I was joking! It was really great, and I was really happy to do it for *you*," hoping it would fix it, more than partly because I really hadn't meant it, after what we had just done together, and the unexpectedly great pleasure I'd received from it.

But she continued to look despondent.

"No, you're right. While I hope you're not lying, and that you did enjoy me, ultimately, you didn't know anything about me before we started having sex, and we both know that you're only doing this, and all you went through tonight because you feel like you financially have to, and we only do it because we can afford to, and are too lazy or afraid to look for people who will make love with us, particularly with kink, because they truly love us." I didn't know what to say, because what she was saying was certainly true in my case.

While I had certainly had amazing recent sexual experiences that I could have never imagined, and that I never would have had otherwise, none of it would ever have happened had I not been desperate for money. Finally, I responded.

"Well, I have no reason to think you unlovable, and you're certainly great at sex, in my limited experience, at least with women. And you've certainly been very good and kind to me, even ignoring the sex. Before tonight, if it is night, I'd never made love with any woman, but I've really enjoyed it, not just with you but the others as well.

"Maybe in your case, you should just think of it as a very expensive way of dating. But if you're looking for a guy, maybe another establishment would be more productive?"

My last words were offered with another smile. After a few seconds, as she thought, she smiled too.

"I'm sorry. I shouldn't have burdened you with my own issues, that you can't possibly understand, partly because perhaps I don't even understand them myself. I just wanted to thank you, because I think you were great, and are a wonderful young woman, and I feel very badly about what that asshole did to you, and that you have to do such things to make ends meet. So to speak."

"OK."

Smiling at the final joke, but realizing now that I wanted to decomplicate the conversation, I continued to slowly come down from my post-climax glow.

"Thank you, too."

It felt kind of weird to be having this discussion, so personally intimate for both of us, in front of a lot of strangers.

And as it was occurring, I continued to remain firmly bound to the platform on which all had happened to me – the two enemas, the first vaginal fucking as my anus was stretched, the tasting of the women, the complete end to my anal virginity. I was still completely exposed, naked and wide and vulnerable between my legs, my feet still strapped and tied behind my head, my arms still tightly bound in front of my spread thighs.

But wordlessly, and seemingly sadly, she finally got off the bench. She stood up, released the harness that had so pleasured both of us from around her waist, pulled it down to her feet, and stepped out of it. She slowly withdrew the equipment from each of the orifices between her own legs, and set them down. Then, as she put on her clothing, and departed with no further conversation, and I looked around, I suddenly realized that very few of the strangers actually were remaining.

The show, such as it was, seemed to be largely over, and the crowd seemed to have mostly dissipated, and I also realized that in our mutual passionate and focused love-making, I hadn't noticed that the sounds of the previously loud anal orgy behind me had ended as well.

I looked around and saw Esmeralda, who had apparently completed the anal servicing of her own last patron, quietly talking to the man who had initially unsuccessfully bid for me, and later rescued me and had, in the end, wanted to take me last. As they spoke, I remained completely immobilized, other than my head, my vagina and anus still stuffed with the vibrator and plug, with continuing suction on my nipples.

And I was still fully exposed and totally vulnerable to whomever wanted to do whatever with me.

But despite being just as firmly bound and bereft of clothing as before, I no longer *felt* naked and powerless – the continuing glow in my full lower orifices from the most-recent orgasms made me feel instead radiant and empowered.

Hours ago, in what now seemed like a previous life, I had deeply dreaded the prospect of a male member entering and stretching my tight exit. But now, having conquered the large vibrator, I lusted for it, and was enthralled that men lusted to do it to me as well.

Now, rather than a helpless vessel for their lust, I was feeling like an erotic Greek goddess on an altar, to be adulated with their eyes and genitals. Eyes closed as I eagerly awaited my last patron, I started to daydream that not just two, but a dozen men had bid for me, and were lined up to worshipfully stuff their firm thick warm meat deep into my rectum, stroking in and out as the tight muscles of my wide taut sphincter squeezed it, urging the helpless offering of hot jets of their semen deep into my otherwise empty bowels, still cleansed from my earlier enemas.

But my latest reverie was interrupted as I felt the vibrator slowly sliding out of my vagina. I opened my eyes to see Esmeralda silently, as usual, setting it aside.

She released the suction on the nipple suckers, and removed them from my breasts. For the first time since the intermission, she loosened the ratchets on the tethers binding my wrists.

Then, for the first time since I had regained consciousness after the abduction, I felt the soft but firm cuffs on my wrists being completely detached from the tethers, and I could, at least for the moment, do whatever I wanted with my hands.

18

=====

THE REDEMPTION

For the first time since I'd awoken from the sedation, I had the full use of my hands, now freed from the tethers that had bound my wrists to the platform on which I'd spent the entire surreal experience.

But I was confused. I knew I still had one more patron to please, and no longer viewed it as something to be feared, or even as a chore but, rather, now hungered for him to replace the plug in my rectum with what I hoped was his hard warm thick penis. As I felt Esmeralda now slowly and gently untying the ropes binding my feet together and to the post behind me, I asked her, quietly, "Does he want me in a different position?"

"Yes. He wants you in a very, very different position. In fact, he wants you in an entirely different location. He wants to take you home with him, and to make passionate love with you with no time limits, and in privacy. Though it's not his fault, he feels guilty that he didn't bid more for you during the intermission; he would have been able to prevent what happened if he had outbid the man who so mindlessly and cruelly beat you.

"We have no objection. As far as we are concerned, since he is happy with that, you have fulfilled your contract with us, and we are happy to call it a night ourselves, though you yourself are not quite done.

"I suppose that if you don't satisfy him, there would be business repercussions for us, but I've come to trust you, and don't expect that to happen. You would in fact be a fool to not do so."

I was a little shocked at the words and, for some reason, after all I'd been through, though I continued to be profoundly grateful to him for saving me, and still recalled the pleasure and emotions of his recent passionate kiss, I found the notion a little disquieting.

As I thought about it, she continued.

"Dora will be bringing you your clothing and belongings presently, and your pay, and Nora will provide you with more pain medication to take now or with you if you need it. With the addition of the unexpected combat compensation, the total will be ten thousand dollars, in benjamins. We won't ask you for a W-9, so there will be no tax consequences, unless you decide to report it to the IRS yourself."

The final words were delivered with a smile.

I was pleasantly shocked at the number, now twice as much as I had initially expected to receive. It made me realize that each of those who had won the bids for me must have paid many thousands of dollars for the privilege of fucking my ass, if the asshole who had beaten me had paid twelve thousand, and wasn't even the highest bidder.

And the woman who had just so enthusiastically and pleasurably fucked me had been the highest one. I couldn't even start to imagine the kind of wealth that would allow someone to spend it so seemingly frivolously, with so many likely free or at least lower-cost anuses out there in the world in which to insert penises, when I couldn't even pay my student loans.

She saw my shock at the number, and perhaps read my mind, as she continued to unbind me.

"They aren't paying to merely fuck a woman in the arse, you see. That is not a dime a dozen, but every woman, and even man, if one is so inclined, has one, and it can certainly be provided for a lot less than they bid for you. We aren't merely selling sex here. Again, anyone can do that. As at Disney, they are paying for an entire experience."

I thought about it, and realized that it had been quite an elaborate production overall, no doubt requiring a great deal of equipment, preparation, planning, practice, rehearsal, and talent, in which I had indeed been a reluctant star performer. As I considered it, she finally freed my feet, unclipped the ankle cuffs from each other, then removed them entirely. I could now lower my legs to the platform as I relaxed with them stretched before me, together for the first time, then hanging over the edge. Still naked, I leaned back against the post to which my feet had been tied for so long. As I did so, she went on.

"Of course, he may provide you with an additional generous tip as well, if he finds you pleasing."

At her words, I suddenly realized why I had felt disturbed about going home with him, and once again broke down in tears. The beautiful woman, who I had earlier thought was heartless, but had later learned was completely the opposite, looked confused once again at her new apparently lachrymose charge, whom surely she must have finally decided was an emotional hot mess.

This time, she really didn't understand, but once again, she tenderly took a cloth to my wet face.

"What is it?"

I was very glad that she didn't add the word "now" to the query, particularly because I could sense that she wanted to. I didn't know how to answer her in any complicated way, so I did so simply, because I knew the answer, though I feared offending her.

"I feel like a whore," I sobbed.

Hearing the words, her response wasn't offense but, as when I'd asked her about how women taste, more beautiful musical laughter.

Then, understanding I was serious, she spoke gently.

"Oh, dear. Darling."

She tenderly took my head in her hands once more, and gave me another long, loving kiss. Finally removing her warm sweet lips from mine, she continued to hold and then hugged me, pressing her warm bare breasts against my own, and rubbing my back. She finally spoke as she continued to gently embrace me.

"If you were worried about that, you should have been worried about it long before now. It should have prevented you from agreeing to the contract with us at all. Regardless of how much you may have enjoyed aspects of it – and as we told you, we generally enjoy them very much – whatever your need or motivations, you have fundamentally done nothing here other than offering sex for pay.

"You may have wanted to think that all of the elaboration, or being bound and having no control over the specifics somehow changed that, but it didn't in any way, because you did it completely voluntarily. You were ultimately in control. You could have ended it at any time, and yet, ignoring the vicious and totally unplanned assault on you due to our own negligence, you did not."

As she spoke, I knew she was right. From when I'd agreed to the contract, all through the "performance," I'd been trying to pretend to myself that I wasn't selling or, at least, renting my body, but of course I had been.

"There are no bright lines in the interactions and transactions between men and women, or humans in general. We are all quite complicated creatures.

"Broadly, no pun intended, women have something for which most men have an innate desperate desire, and enjoy providing it. Men also have things that women need, and generally like to provide them as well, particularly when they receive the unique services of the woman in exchange.

"In the end, other than in degree, how does what you did today, or even are about to do, differ from having sex with a man after he bought you an expensive dinner on a first date, other than perhaps the lack of explicitness of the contractual arrangement?

"They call prostitution 'the world's oldest profession,' but really, it is an absurd notion that didn't exist before the existence of cash, or at least currency. And we're going to provide you with some, regardless of the location of your previous or future amorous or otherwise copulatory activities, and he may as well, in addition. And if he does, it changes nothing.

"There are many other ways in which he could compensate you for his sexual gratification. One of them could even be marriage. That is, traditionally, the way in which society has legitimized these exchanges. And for all I know, he may even offer it. Crazier things have happened. There has even been at least one Hollywood film about such a thing, I believe.

"But please don't delude yourself that anything changes because he has paid to stuff his stiff prick into your now-trained arse, or does anything else to you in his own bed, rather than here, bound to our equipment.

"And one more request. Please stop crying so much. Please. You'll be fine," she finished, but with another smile.

As she lectured me, I realized that, again, she was right. I had imagined that what I'd been doing up to now wasn't wrong, but what I was about to do was, but they couldn't be ethically separated. And right or wrong, I was about to be well compensated for what I'd done and gone through and the only barrier to getting the full compensation was to foolishly create such an illogical separation.

As we had been talking, and I had been crying, the other women had appeared with my clothes, the medication, and my purse, with the cash. Dora carefully counted it out for me, a hundred hundred-dollar bills, as I watched. My tears now dry, Esmeralda spoke again.

"Here are your clothes. Put them on, but keep your plug in your arse for him. Consider it a small parting gift from us, or part of your compensation," she smiled.

The latter words seemed crass, but made perfect sense in the context of her lecture. Fortunately, my clothing was simple: my underwear, yoga pants, the bra, and the sweatshirt, with sandals. It didn't take long. Except as I tried to pull on the sweatshirt, the last garment, I struggled to get the thick wrist cuffs through the tighter sleeves, and couldn't see how to do it with them on.

"May I remove the cuffs to get my sweatshirt on?"

"No.

"Or rather, if you can't get it on with the cuffs attached, then we'll take them off briefly, but they will have to be put back on you before you leave. They are a necessary part of completing your contract."

I raised my eyebrows in curiosity.

"Normally, we would rebind and blindfold you to deliver you to a neutral location to release you, and perhaps even sedate you again in a similar manner to that in which you were brought here. You must understand that we are quite serious about outsiders not knowing our location.

"Fortunately for you, because we trust your last patron, having much experience with him, he will do that for us. Once you are clothed, your hands will be recuffed behind your back, and you will be blindfolded, and he will take you to his home, and what happens after that is up to the two of you. He is actually simplifying our standard process for us, which is the main reason we are allowing this."

Now understanding, I nodded. She removed the cuffs, and I pulled on the shirt. Then she put them back on my wrists, as tightly as before.

"Now," she commanded, "hands behind your back. Spit spot."

I felt like I was being ordered around by some sort of beautiful kinky Mary Poppins. Standing and fully clothed now, for the first time in hours, I put my arms behind me, and felt her clip the cuffs on my wrists together. Then I felt her place something into my cuffed hands.

"All right, here is your purse, with the money."

She walked around in front of me. "It is now time to blindfold you, so you can go with him, and then get on with the rest of your life."

Before she could do it, tears started to well in my eyes again. She could see it as she was about to apply the blindfold to me, and this time, she actually did ask, in a tone with a hint of exasperation, "All right, what now?"

"I'm going to miss you."

I started to sob again.

"I know it sounds crazy, after everything that's happened, but I hate that I'll never see any of you again. Even him."

The last words came as I saw him standing nearby, in silence.

"I sort of feel like it was wrong in some sense, but I'm not sure why, and this has been the most amazing experience of my life, and you all helped me through it."

"It's called the 'Stockholm Syndrome,'" Dora brightly chirped. "You bonded to us because we bondaged you."

"Oh, that's silly, Dora." Nora's tone was annoyed.

"This isn't about psychology, or hostages. It's just that she had a lot of great sex, and we got to know and like each other, even though it's only been a few hours."

Then she came up and gave me a hug, with one more deep long kiss. As she finally pulled away, she whispered quietly in my ear, "What I said about enjoying inflicting pain? That was just part of the act. I don't really, and I like you. But I do want to be an actress."

I smiled at the words. "I think you're a great one."

She beamed in response.

Apparently chastened by Nora's admonition, Dora came up and sweetly kissed me as well. "We don't get many like you. You were really fun."

"Can you please hug me? I want to hug you, but I can't."

She wrapped her arms around me, embracing me tightly and, like Esmeralda, pressing her soft warm naked breasts against my own now-clothed ones, gave me another kiss, then slowly released me and backed away.

I looked over at him, as he stared at me for a moment. Then he came over, grabbed me in his strong arms, as my hands continued to be bound behind me holding my pay in my purse, and dipped me, with his own deep passionate kiss. I offered no resistance as he took his mouth in mine, just as I hadn't with the women.

"It was a performance."

The words came as he gradually lifted me back vertical and pulled his lips away from mine after a minute or so. His tone was completely different than it had ever been previously, and he finally, for the first time since the show had begun, addressed me in the second person.

"You were magnificent, even with the disobedience and punishment. In fact, it greatly enhanced the performance, even if it didn't enhance your own experience. I didn't want to really hurt you, and hope that you don't think I was deliberately cruel, and I fervently hope that you get everything you want in life going forward."

I thought a bit before responding.

"I did think you were cruel, and heartless. I thought she was, too. I didn't understand the nature of what was happening, and perhaps my lack of knowledge improved the performance at the time, but I do understand it now."

I hesitated. "I almost used the safe phrase when you were tickling my feet. I didn't think I could take much more."

His reply came with no hesitation.

"Yes, I know.

"I could sense it; it's why I stopped when I did. I am always very careful in such delicate matters, if possible and I can tell, to not go too far. It would have spoiled the show, and your own prospects. That I could tell is a compliment to you."

Shocked at the words, again realizing the degree of talent that had gone into what I now considered our production, and how close I had come to losing all, I thought about it for a bit.

"Thank you."

He nodded.

After a pause, I repeated, "Really. Thank you very much. I'm good. I'm in fact great. And you are, too."

He finally smiled in response.

Finally, I looked back at her. At this point, it almost felt like the end of *The Wizard of Oz*, as though I had suddenly re-met old friends, thinking "...*and you were there, and you were there, and...*" She spoke.

"I know it sounds silly, but as you can see by the others' reactions, you are indeed special."

It was a little weird, almost like the blonde good witch, who had the same name. Except then from some remnant of a misspent youth I realized that the blonde good witch had been Glinda, not Esmeralda. The latter was actually a Disney princess.

Which made almost as much sense, given the production values of the establishment. That is, if you ignored the appalling lack of current family values.

But I really felt very confident that Disney would not produce a veritable movie about what I had just gone through in less than fifteen years from now. Beyond that, I really couldn't be sure.

Almost certainly having no idea of the rapid and perverse popular-culture thoughts going through my mind, she looked at me for a few moments, then tenderly embraced me as well, my hands still cuffed behind me.

She then gave me one more perfunctory, not passionate, kiss on each cheek and first hesitatingly, then enthusiastically whispered in my ear. "If you ever want to talk, my email address is..."

It was a gmail address, with no special characters, and it was thoroughly memorable.

"Because I like you, too. If you really want, I know how to get in touch with the others," she winked, with a final smile. With the words, she nodded to my final patron, and he came over as she finally, and this time, actually seemingly sadly, applied my blindfold, the last bit of my bondage from her.

As I stood there and she departed herself from my view with the temporary end of my vision, I could see him no longer, either. But I heard him.

"I'll carry and protect your money for you for now. You can trust me with it; I can assure you that I have no personal need for it."

I silently let him take the purse from me, then he took my left cuffed hand behind me in his own right and, gently and seemingly lovingly holding it, guided me out of the chamber in which I had spent the most seemingly consequential hours of my life.

Unable to see, walking a little funny with the thick plug still buried in my ass, as we strolled together to his car, wherever it was, both of us holding hands behind my back, he casually asked, "What's your name?"

The normally familiar opening question was in the moment a little jarring. I realized that it was the first time, after being treated as "the subject," "the creature," a sexual lab rat, for so many hours, that anyone had even asked or seemed to care. It also seemed very strange that this man, who had so closely seen me engaged for hours in the most intimate possible physical activities between my legs, didn't know something so basic about me but, of course, how would he, how could he have?

But hearing the question, finally, it also made me feel like my life was starting to become normal again. I felt like we could start anew. I stated it simply, almost as in kinder-garten.

"My name is Lisa. What is yours?"

His response was even more simple.

"It's Derek."

"What happens next, Derek?"

He seemed to think for a bit as we continued to walk, then I heard him speak.

"Well, all right, but be patient with me; after the past few hours, I may have to slowly transition into this. What happens next, is that after my darling Lisa and I get to my car, which is just a few steps ahead of us, I will take my darling Lisa home."

He continued, as he gently escorted me to the passenger door, opened it, then helped me get into the seat.

"Once there, I will remove my darling Lisa's blindfold and uncuff her, unless she actually likes being blindfolded and cuffed, a possibility I don't entirely exclude."

He shut my door and I heard him walk around and get in on the driver's side. I felt him reach around over my right shoulder and pull down and safely fasten my belt as my hands remained cuffed behind me. Foolishly, I had thought the bondage over, but apparently I had been wrong.

"After that," he went on, as he started the engine of what sounded like a very expensive and powerful machine, "My darling Lisa will regain ownership of her body, and we will make gentle passionate love, in whatever way she tells me that she actually enjoys it, without being helplessly bound and spread in front of dozens of strangers and being treated like a laboratory animal. And then my darling Lisa and I will both decide what happens after that.

"I will do whatever the subject wants me to do, at least in the near term. I may, ultimately, and it may not take that long, even address the subject in the second person."

I played along as, my hands still cuffed behind me and blindfolded, I finally felt the car hit the road on the way to his home and, perhaps, who knew, what might even ultimately become my own.

"OK, I'm pretty sure that your darling Lisa will enjoy that, Derek, baby. I know her pretty well, and I think she will like that very much."

And this time, whatever the second person or third person might think about that, I was now pretty confident that the first person would.